GRAFFITI
GRANDMA

JO BARNEY

D1533947

ISBN: 0615726453

ISBN-13: 9780615726458

Library of Congress Control Number: 2012953450

Encore Press Portland, OR

www.JoBarneyWrites.com

This is for the thousands of kids who've lost their families and who go out to look for them, or something to take their place, on the mean streets of every city everywhere

CHAPTER ONE

SARAH

SEPTEMBER 2009

I can remember every second of that last graffiti patrol with Ellie. Maybe it's the meds they're feeding me, or maybe I'm a little crazy right now. The nurse says I probably should be with all the stuff I've gone through in the past couple of weeks, Ellie at the center of it all.

It was chilly that morning, and we shivered a little as we headed toward the first mailbox, me, in my punk clothes, Ellie in her old lady sweatshirt and red sneakers. She had her supplies and towels in an old shopping bag, like usual, and I could tell she was still mad at me, at my knowing how the graffiti got on the boxes. I was thinking about that, too, but she didn't know the whole story, not then.

"Spray!" Ellie ordered, and I stopped remembering and pointed the bottle at the mailbox in front of me. We scrubbed, Ellie not talking to me yet. After a couple of minutes, the black polish on my nails began to melt like the paint scrawls we were working on. Ellie muttered "Good" when she saw me rubbing at them. As soon as the box was as clean as Graffiti X could get it, we headed toward the next one. By the time we got to the street with the big trees, I was getting hot and glad for what little shade was left, the limbs above me almost bare. Leaves crunched under my boots.

The people who lived in these buildings were rich. I could tell by the doors, the polished brass knobs, and the pots of flowers beside them. They must sit on their upstairs terraces and feel like they were living in the arms of the trees. I was imagining eating breakfast four stories up and feeding a squirrel a piece of pancake, when I stumbled and heard the heel of my boot snap. *Shit, my only shoes* was my first thought. I had to walk like a cripple, one leg short, one long.

"Take 'em off!" Ellie said, shaking her gray head at me. "Stupid to wear boots like that; you look like a baby hooker." She took the bag of supplies from me, and I leaned against a tree and pulled them off. The cold from the sidewalk seeped through the leaves and into my toes. The look on Ellie's face told me not to complain, so I shoved the boots into the bag. Maybe I could get the heel fixed somewhere. "We'll finish up with the next box. When we get back you can borrow a pair of my old sneakers."

I watched where I was going, hoping I wouldn't step on dog poop or something yucky hidden under the leaves. That's when I saw the white basketball shoe sticking up from a pile of debris at the curb. Someone must have lost it. Except that the shoe also had a sock in it. And in the sock, a leg.

I grabbed Ellie's arm and pointed. She looked, made a sound like she was choking. I ran to the gutter and pushed sticks and leaves away from the rest of the leg. I saw familiar, worn denim jeans, recognized a plaid patch on a thigh, a hand I knew because of the small ink tattoo of a smiley face at the wrist. I was bawling by the time I uncovered his head, brushed bits of dirt from his eyes, understood that he was dead. Peter.

"Leave him!" Ellie yanked on my arm, her words daggers of icy fear. "Not our business." She had me up on my feet, and I shoved at her and knocked her into the trunk of a tree. "It's trouble!" She reached for me again. "Nothing good ever comes from a dead body." I was crying so hard I couldn't see. She grabbed my arm and pulled me through the trail of leaves. "I'll call 911," she said. "When we get home. Anonymous."

And she did, and now I'm lying here in this hospital bed hoping she's still alive.

CHAPTER TWO

ELLIE

SEPTEMBER 2009

I'm muttering ancient thoughts when I notice the girl standing on the corner, looking at me. Black boots, net stockings, holes at the knees, a tacky black skirt under a fat jacket, its elbows patched. Her black hair looks plastic, her dark-rimmed eyes shiny blue.

She cocks her head at me like a curious crow. She frowns. "Hey! That was really pretty."

"Beauty is in the eye of the beholder," I say. I keep scrubbing.

"So you're hired by the government or something?"

I wave her out of the way with one hand and spray another swoosh of Graffiti X on the silver lines. This time I'll wait the thirty seconds before I get worked up. "No," I answer.

"Oh, so you just do it?"

The midnight artists have attacked the mailbox in front of me until their fat pens and sprayers and brushes have created a gruesome mass of internal organs, a handful of spindly fingers, an eyeball or two, and some scary, foreign-looking scribbles.

"Yes." I pass the steel wool over the metal fingers, and the pad etches its way into the black letters I am uncovering. VAGINA. Just when did that become a dirty word? I press harder. The girl has moved behind me, is watching the body parts, the body word, disintegrate.

I make a final swipe at the edges of the box, push against a curve of silver that still shows. I'm woozy from the smell of the damp rag, and my fingers on my right hand are up to the knuckles in black and silver goop, too late for gloves.

"That's it for this one," I say in the girl's direction, meaning good-bye. I turn and head for the next mailbox, a block away. I hear her boots tapping on the sidewalk behind me. High heels, for God's sake. She's, like, what? Fifteen?

Most of the time, people don't even look at me as I scrub. Sometimes someone will ask if I get paid. After a glance at my apron, the grungy red Kmart sneakers swallowing my anklets, the nubs of gray hair escaping from under my Yankees baseball cap, the questioner usually smiles in an embarrassed way and hurries off.

One time a little kid asked me, after I told him to stand back and don't breathe in what I'm spraying, if I was a grandma. I said no, because I'm not sure. "I think you're Graffiti Grandma," he said, pulling his lip down over his teeth so he couldn't take in my poison. His mother yelled at him, and I never saw him again, but the title has stuck in my head. Could be worse.

"Can I help?"

"Why would you want to?" The girl's finger, or the finger of a midnight buddy, pressing down on a button, has created the blue organ, the yellow eye, the dangerous word, and now she's watching an old lady clean up after them. She'll have a good story to tell her gang the next time they come around with their cans of paint and felt pens and whatever they swallow or sniff to get their artistic juices running.

She comes closer to me, takes the shopping bag from me with one hand and my elbow with the other. "I'm Sarah," she says.

"I don't care who you are." I shake her off and grab the bag back. "I can do this myself." For a second, I could swear I was talking back to my grandmother. I stop walking and consider that thought.

All my life I have lived by that motto and I'm not going to change now, despite the lines of silver paint pen refusing to melt into my wads of paper. Or maybe because of them. Life has presented me with any number of stubborn uglinesses, and early on I learned that they are best faced alone. Especially when the would-be helper looks, with her black eyes, duct-taped black jacket, and ragged skirt, like the spawn of a failed witch and a raccoon.

"And where has it got me?" I didn't mean the question for her, but she shrugs, a little grin moving her lips. I know the answer: a door punched into an olive green hallway like twenty other doors, behind which old people like me fall apart. What the hell. "I'm Ellie," I say. I hand her the bag and we head to the next corner.

I choose, for reasons of my own and which I am not too clear about, to go out each week and clean up the U.S. mail receptacles bolted to the sidewalks lining the four blocks around my apartment house. It's one of the few things I can still choose. Something inside me makes me attack those blue boxes, even though at times I grumble so loud dogs growl as they sniff at my shoes, my stained bag, their owners saying sorry, yanking their animals and themselves away. I don't know why I get so worked up. And I've tried to understand it, the graffiti, the why of it, the need to signal that someone's been there on walls, signs, and mailboxes, like dogs do on tree trunks.

On this next box, a red heart wraps around a word: MOM. This isn't the first time I've come across this valentine, and it puzzles me almost as much as VAGINA. "What would that person's mother think if she knew her kid was vandalizing public property in her name?" I ask my helper.

The girl squirts the bottle a couple of times, and the soft red crayon melts fast, drips in bloody splatters onto the cement. "Maybe that kid doesn't have a mom," she answers as she bends over and tries to mop up the sidewalk.

I wipe fast while the red's still melting. The box's blue enamel comes out almost clean. "So he doesn't have to worry about what she'll think?"

Sarah blinks, looks away. "Where to next?" she asks. We turn the corner.

This block is lined with classy apartments and new condos. The only old things the developer left after tearing out a couple of decrepit mansions are the eighty-year-old trees, maples and oaks, lining the street. Their used-up leaves play in the cool fall air, pad our steps. Sarah scuffs her boots through the dry drifts, trying to leave a track, maybe, so she can find her way back. That's what I used to think when my son, Danny, headed off to first grade scuffing the same way, me standing at the door watching.

"Over there." I point at the backs of a row of shoulder-high parking signs. "Easy targets for anyone wanting to make his mark in the world."

At some point, in the months I've been cleaning up my neighborhood, I came to the conclusion that's why kids tag. Maybe it's because I myself once wanted to make a mark in the world.

She's already got the spray bottle out, and she aims it at the scribbles running across a PARKING 10 MINUTES sign. Black ink sags onto the rag in her hand. "I think this is making a mark *on* the world, not *in* it."

"Would you please explain that to the jerks who are doing it?"

The girl steps back, wipes a finger across an eyelid, maybe squinting against the sting of Graffiti X. "You think I do this stuff?"

I've heard this question before. Danny, about her age: "You think I do this stuff?" Even now, I can feel my hand reaching into his pocket, touching the plastic bag, pulling it out, the white crystals rustling inside. I can still hear myself yell, "Get out."

"Yes," I say. She's slipped out of her fat jacket and has tied it around her waist by the sleeves. She looks like she's being hugged by an elephant. The arm that brushes mine is tattooed. A flower winds from elbow to shoulder, reds and oranges and greens. I poke a finger at a blossom. "Anybody who could do this to herself is capable of doing the same to a mailbox."

She gives up the bag when I pull at it. I toss the bottle in and head toward the last box on my route. I don't look back, but I imagine she's standing on the curb, glancing around, wondering who else to bother.

That first time, I believed Danny when he said, "Trust me." I let him stay for another year, until the night he left for good, me bloody, hanging on to a doorjamb and screaming, "You're not my son anymore." We both were screwed up, me on cheap bourbon, Danny on who-knows-what. He never did come back home. The one time he called, I told him I couldn't help him. It was up to him, just like it was up to me, to find our separate ways. So far, I told him, I am not good at saving myself, much less other people.

"Thanks a lot, Mom." Ugly words, worse than cussing at me, words I kept hearing while I made my way to clean and sober. Last summer one of his high school buddies told me he saw Danny up north in

Green River. "Looks good," he said. "He was haul-
ing around a little kid in a pack on his chest. Gavin,
I think his name was." I should be glad for that news,
both of us finding our ways, even if Gavin is one
more son to regret not knowing.

I lift my foot to avoid catching the loose sole of
my shoe on a root-raised hunk of sidewalk. The city
needs to come fix stuff like that, I think, probably out
loud. I can see the last box half a block away, Day-
Glo green swirls signaling to me. I shut my mouth,
walk a little faster, not wanting to think about unfix-
able upheavals elsewhere.

Then I hear Sarah's voice floating toward me like
the leaves dropping from the trees. "The freesia's
for my mom. She liked to grow them." I stop, turn
around, see her leaning against the clean mailbox,
wiping her eyes on a jacket sleeve, her face disappearing into her hands.

I pat my pants pocket, feel a fold of Kleenex, take
a step, then another, toward her. I can't stand watching someone cry.

"I grew freesias once," I call to her.

CHAPTER THREE

JEFFREY

1986-1991

The only thing Jeffrey can remember about his mother is that she has red lips. Whenever the five-year-old sees a red-lipped woman on the street, on the bus, or on his father's arm, he wants to run up and take her hand in his, but he is too big to hold hands, his father told him, giving him a knock on the head the last time he did it. The woman had smiled at him, but he could see that it wasn't his mother because this lady's teeth were shiny with gold.

He and his father live on the first floor of an apartment house, and they sleep on the sofa that is opened into a bed most of the time. Sometimes his father has a visitor, and then Jeffrey takes a pillow into the closet and sleeps among the shoes and wad of clothes that have been tossed inside to make the room neat for the visitor. Sometimes the visitor has red lips, but she is never his mother. Finally, his father tells him to stop being so fuckin' stupid the morning he can't stop crying after he finds a lady sleeping crosswise on the sofa, her hair touching the floor, her red lipstick smeared like jam across her face.

Jeffrey understands then that his mother is gone, for sure. "Off somewhere, the bitch." The way his father says it, his hand flinging out and bumping into the bottle that lives on the table, the boy knows two things: his father hates his mother, and his father will hit him if he asks one more time.

Sometimes he wishes he could live at school with his kindergarten teacher, Mrs. Michaels. She smiles and pats his shoulder and teaches him songs like "Itsy Bitsy Spider," which Jeffrey sings to himself as he walks home and waits for his father to come in. One night he waits until it is dark, and he gets hungry so he spoons peanut butter into his mouth and pours orange juice into a cup, careful not to spill. The bed is open and when he gets tired, he crawls in between the lump of covers.

The next morning he wakes up and wonders if he should go to school because it is light outside. He is sure Mrs. Michaels will miss him if he doesn't come, so he heads down the street and finds the playground empty and the big doors locked. He sings his way home, pulls the key on the string out from under his T-shirt, and puts it in the lock like usual.

At the lock's click, the door swings open and a hand reaches out, sweeps across his head. He feels himself flying first up and then down, and he lands on his nose, his face pressed into the rug.

"Little jerk. Had me worried. Don't ever disappear like that . . . " His father's voice falls apart and his body crumples on top of Jeffrey. It is a long time before Jeffrey can dig himself out from under the weight of arms and legs and chest and the smell of beer and make his way to the sofa.

Five years later, his father doesn't come home all night or all day. The first few hours alone, Jeffrey is glad his father isn't around. He smoothes the blanket on the couch and begins to read for the third time his favorite book, *The Incredible Journey*, the turning of its pages the only sound in the quiet apartment.

He's not afraid to be alone, but he is a little worried because the bread bag is empty. He uses his finger as a bookmark and lays the book on his chest. What would happen to him if his dad doesn't show up for a long time? No way could he be on his own. Ten years old is like being a baby. Not like the teenagers on the street below who push him around and grab his jacket looking for money or candy. Those guys can take care of themselves, their dark shades and tattoos protecting them like the combat armor on the soldiers in the news. Nobody messes with them. He wishes he had a pair of sunglasses.

The buzzer startles him. "It's all right," a voice says, and he presses the button to let her through the front door. Minutes later, a fat lady with a plastic ID tag around her neck walks in and tells him to pack up his clothes and, glancing at the book in his hand, perhaps a favorite book. "Your father won't be home for a while," she says. "We have a very nice foster family who will take care of you in the meantime."

In the meantime lasts until the trial is over. Mrs. Oscar, a social worker, he has learned, arrives and tells him to pack up again, he is going home. His grandfather is coming to take custody of him. "You are lucky to have a family member willing to take that responsibility. Some kids don't."

Jeffrey looks around the small room that has been his for the past three weeks. What grandfather? He can smell dinner cooking, can hear his foster mother Helen tell the two other kids to wash up and be quick about it. Before he piles his clothes into the bag, he makes sure the bed is neat. That is one of Helen's rules. She has a lot of rules, and he likes the way her rules make him feel safe, like streetcar tracks that know the way.

"Come along."

In the car, Jeffrey learns that his father has been sentenced to ten years in the state penitentiary after pleading guilty to armed robbery and the attempted murder of a Chinese man who ran the corner market. "Your grandfather is coming in an hour on the train from Las Vegas. He'll be here soon."

"I didn't know I had a grandfather."

"Really!" Mrs. Oscar looks at her watch. "I have another appointment in a few minutes. Will you be all right alone for a little while once I get you settled back at your apartment?"

"I guess," Jeffrey says, still feeling the hug Helen gave him when she said good-bye. Maybe he could visit her once in a while? Mrs. Oscar shrugs, says maybe, and Jeff knows he probably won't.

After she leaves, he opens his book, but he's read it too many times. He looks out the window. The mean guys are still there, but he sees someone moving through the tangle of legs and hoodies on the steps. The man, big in an overcoat and hat, takes a piece of paper from his pocket and then climbs up to the apartment house's entry door. A second later, the buzzer rings, and Jeff picks up the intercom earpiece.

"Yeah," he says, not knowing that word is leading him into the next chapter of his life.

"It is I," a voice announces. "Your grandfather."

"Stupid," the old man says once he's gotten into the flat and explains himself. "Your father always was stupid. Never went to school unless the principal threatened no lunch if he didn't come often enough, and that only lasted until he found ways to get free lunch without having to go to school. But first, let's find somewhere to eat."

"Dad got free lunch?" Jeffrey asks, his mouth full of hamburger bun. He knows what that is, and he gets it, too, every day. He just didn't know his father also had to put up with the eye-rolling classmates who pay for their food with weekly checks, not the blue ticket his teacher gives him that makes him less a kid than they are.

"Why?" he asks. His and his grandfather's fingers touch as they reach for fries on the tray between them.

"We had very little money. I hurt my back on a job and was on workman's comp. Mildred, your grandmother, was a good woman, but she died early. So it was Bucky and I on our own. We did quite well for a while, but he probably blamed me for the loss of his mother. That's why, when he grew up, he left." His grandfather's watery eyes look out the window. Then he turns and smiles. "And now I'm here, meeting my grandson for the first time."

Jeffrey asks again, "Why?"

The old man takes Jeffrey's hand, his touch soft and unfamiliar. "Your father not only found ways to make money outside the usual accepted ways, but he also found ways to spend it."

Jeffrey's savior has gray hair combed in neat ridges across his head, and his bright hooded eyes look at Jeffrey in a way he isn't used to, into him, it seems like. His grandfather talks different, too, quiet, every word coming out like it is being tasted. Jeffrey listens hard, trying to understand what he is hearing. It isn't that he doesn't get the words, despite some of them that slip right by him; it is just the opposite. It seems like he understands more than the old man is saying, his voice sounding just the way a person would imagine a grandfather's voice would be: low, tangled with laughter and sadness, a rope flung to a foundering boy. Foundering. His grandfather uses that word to describe Jeffrey, and he knows what it means even without knowing.

"What should I call you?" Jeffrey asks.

"Grandpa Jack. Does that suit you? And, if it's okay with you, I'd like to call you Jeff. New names for our new life together."

Over the next couple of days, the two of them clean out the apartment, throw away most of the stuff that fills the drawers and the floor of the closet, and call Goodwill to pick up the furniture they won't be using in their new place. During the packing and sorting and tossing, Grandpa Jack talks and Jeff listens until he feels okay about asking about some things that are bothering him. "How come I never met you before?" Then, even before Grandpa Jack can answer, "What did my father do that made you not want to be around him?"

By the time their work is finished, Jeff has learned that his father was a thug and a drug dealer early on, and when Grandpa Jack called his son on it, he moved out, lived a dissolute life (his grandfather paused, explained "lawless, lost" when Jeff frowned) until he met Kathi, Jeff's mother. Kathi was into drugs, but not bad. She meant well, kept their apartment clean, cooked every once in a while. When she got pregnant, she stopped the drugs and laid down the law with Bucky. She told him, who, proud of his woman, then told Grandpa Jack, "We're going to have a normal life, you're going to get a job, I'm going to be a mother, and we're going to have a family."

Grandpa Jack sighs, wipes his lips with his paper napkin. "They almost made it. You were the glue holding Bucky and Kathi together for a few years. Then Kathi got bored with motherhood, and she started using again, and your father, who had taken a job as a school custodian, you were that important to him," he says, pointing a "remember this" finger at Jeff, "flipped out and beat her up when he found her so high that she had left you alone for a day."

Jeff remembers a lot of times he came home to an empty house, but never one empty of his mother. In his memory, his red-lipped mother never left him until the day she left forever.

"I was living in Phoenix at the time, glad that Bucky seemed to be shaping up, coming to adulthood in a satisfying way, when I got the letter from Kathi." His grandfather takes a piece of paper from his pocket, presses out its creases, reads. "I'm leaving this town because I've become a bad mother and because your son has beaten me so bad I spent three days in the hospital. If ever Jeffrey needs a family, please take care of him. Of all the things I've done, he's the very, very best." Grandpa Jack passes the note to Jeff, and he sees that his mother had signed it with a heart over the *i* in her name.

Jeff holds the paper in his hand and feels a weight lift from his body. His mother did not leave because she didn't love him. She didn't love his father. He'd hurt her. Who wouldn't leave? Then the next thought lands like a bag of rocks across his shoulders. Why didn't she take him with her? He runs a finger over her name. She loved him. He can feel it, warm as he touches the heart. She was just messed up for a while. She might even be looking for him right now. He glances up, sees Grandpa Jack shaking his head.

"She is dead, Jeff. The drugs."

It is his fault. If she hadn't gotten pregnant, his mother and father wouldn't have gotten married, would just have gone on doing what they were doing, nobody's business. When he was born, he ruined everything. No wonder his father drank so much. No wonder his mother is dead.

Jeff gives the paper back to Grandpa Jack and tries to pay attention to what the old man is saying.

"I wrote to Bucky, when I got the note, that I couldn't condone a man beating up a woman, the mother of his child. I told him I was not his father from that moment on. He was on his own. Good riddance." Grandpa Jack squeezes Jeff's hand. "But I didn't take you into account, Jeff. I thought you'd be with your mother and taken care of. Until a week ago, when Children's Services called and informed me that you needed me." He wraps an arm around Jeff's shoulder. "You and I have a second chance at being a family."

Jeff manages a smile. A second chance. This time he will not mess up.

They move into an apartment a mile away from the old one, and, on his first day outside, on sidewalks that hold only a few old ladies on the porches and a lot of leaves in the gutter, Jeff skateboards into a new friend, Danny.

Grandpa Jack frightens Jeff a little the night he pulls up the bedcovers and slips in beside him. A hand passes over his chest and lies warmly on his penis and after a while, it doesn't seem so strange.

In those first months that they've lived together, his grandfather has told him that he loves him as he rubs his back or massages his legs. He assures Jeff he will never be unsafe again. He is a special boy, Grandpa Jack says, a wonderful grandson who brings happiness to an old man.

"Like now," he says this night, his hand moving a little. "Feels good, doesn't it?"

Jeff says yes.

A few weeks later, Jeff helps his grandfather feel good, too. And when he cries out in pain, Grandpa Jack tells him it is part of growing up, of being a man, and he will be gentle until his body gets used to it. And his body does get used to it, and Jeff begins to sleep on the far edge of his bed and wait for the door to open and the mattress to sink, the covers to be lifted, letting in cold air and his grandfather.

CHAPTER FOUR

MATT TROMMALD

1998-2000

The boy stands motionless, looks through him, as Matt opens the door. "Collin?" His son seems not to have heard him. As Matt reaches out, asks, "How did you get here?" he notices a movement at the elevator. Marge is slipping into its closing doors.

"Wait! What is this?" he calls. Too late.

His fingers on Collin's shoulder brush against a note pinned to the boy's jacket sleeve. Collin has not moved, seems not to be breathing. Pee floods his small Nikes, pools on the hallway carpet. This is how it is with his son when he is afraid.

Matt picks up Collin, who even at seven is small, frail even, and carries him to the bathroom, begins to strip him of his wet trousers. As he tugs on the green jacket's zipper, the boy stiffens, his arms thrash upwards, his face becomes a terrified mask, and the sounds begin. The first time Matt heard that howl, the hairs on the back of his neck raised. Even now, five years later, his son's fear stuns him. For a moment, he can't think of what he is supposed to do. A flailing hand whips past his face, reminds him. He wraps his son in his arms and holds him tight; his *It's okay, buddy*'s disappear into the roar erupting from the prisoner he confines.

When the sounds become gasping sobs, Matt takes Collin into the living room sofa and pulls him onto his lap in front of the television. Collin likes television, the movement, the sounds that divert his attention for long moments. The boy breathes more easily. The tears have left salty white tracks on his cheeks.

Matt unpins the note.

I can't do it anymore, Matt. I am not the mother Collin should have gotten. I am empty of love for him, and I am afraid not only for him, but for myself. He's yours from now on. Don't try to find me. I won't be there. I'm sorry. Marge.

The paper's crumpling brings Collin's head up. His hair brushes Matt's lips, a breath of a kiss, an affection Collin never offers on purpose. Matt tightens his hug, and Collin sinks back against his chest. For the first time in years, Matt wants a drink, badly. Instead, he takes five deep breaths through his nose, as his rehab counselor taught him, and, while the quiet lasts, tries to think what to do.

Marge has moved away, beyond their marriage, beyond the disturbing boy it produced, beyond the divorce that for a while offered each of them a few hours of peace as they passed their child from one to the other like a burning firebrand.

She had gotten the worst of the custody arrangement, of course, spending weekdays and nights driving Collin to treatment and to his special pre-school and attempting to calm his agitation when his clothing itched, when his stuffed toy, a ragged rat, got lost in the blankets, when his class changed rooms and lost him, when the loud noise of a home run at his first and only baseball game stiffened him into a screaming, unmanageable tangle of arms and legs.

Times like those, and many more, also happened on his watch, but Matt always knew that on Monday morning he could tuck his son's clothes into a duffel, get into his patrol car, drop his weekend load at an open door, and get on with his real life as a cop.

However, this warm, still lump in his lap, with its thumb and finger tapping again and again, as they have tapped for years, means that all has changed. At the moment, Matt can't see beyond opening the suitcase propped against the wall in the hall and finding Rat before Collin misses him.

The boy doesn't stir when Matt moves him onto the cushion of the chair. The suitcase holds clothes, Rat, and the vial of meds prescribed to help him sleep. Moments later, Collin swallows the pill with the chocolate milk Matt keeps for him in the fridge, and he lets himself be led into the bedroom he knows as his from the weekends with his father. He wraps his fingers around Rat snuggling at his throat, its tail in his mouth, and that's how Matt leaves his son, the door open a little, hall light on. If the pill works, Matt will have a few hours to try to figure things out.

He needs to take a couple of days off. Nothing important is on his desk at the moment, and unless a new case comes in, he can hand his files to the others, keep in touch by phone. His team will understand. They always have.

He never blamed the drinking or the hell their marriage became on Collin's autism. The falling apart started almost as soon as they got married, the bump not yet visible under her white suit, the truth that they did not love each other also buried under a façade of hope. After Collin was born. Marge changed from a young girl who laughed a lot to a haggard woman who couldn't stop crying. The two of them crept through a black year. Despite the sadness of his mother, the gnawing feeling of helplessness in his father, Collin grew, grinned at them, slept through the night.

Then, slowly, Madge recovered her self, learned to love her son. So did Matt. He didn't understand how much until the night he, a rookie cop, faced a sixteen-year-old whose gun, held by two straight arms like Rambo, was aimed at his badge. Matt yelled a warning three times, his voice, not his own, cracking, and when the frenzied kid kept coming, yelling, "Kill me, kill me, before I kill you," Matt reached for his weapon.

His one shot didn't kill him but sent the teenager into a lifetime of wheelchairs. Weeks later, the review committee's report identified Sammy Williams as bipolar, damaged goods, known to be dangerous when manic. Matt was exonerated by the committee, but not by himself.

Dreams brought sleepless nights. The contorted face, the screaming plea, the blood on the alley's rough pavement, played in an endless loop of guilt he could not stop. Often he dreamed that the injured boy had Collin's fat cheeks, his toothy laugh. He'd wake, go to his son's crib, weep with relief.

Matt started dropping by the cop bar for a few beers, coming home late for dinner to a silent wife, TV his evening companion. Arguments with Marge erupted like flash fires, singeing the air.

Sometime during these unsteady months, Collin morphed from a smiling, talkative two-year-old into a silent, anxious, hyperactive thirty-pound tyrant who specialized in tantrums. He stopped talking. He wouldn't look at his parents or anyone else who talked to him. He began to cringe when they picked him up. Bribes of ice cream could not make him say "Mama," or "Papa," or any other once-familiar word. This silent Collin seemed happiest building block towers, knocking them down, building them up again.

His parents blamed each other.

"If you would only give him a little more attention."

"If you didn't pamper him like an exotic pet."

"If only . . . " They went out of their minds with *if only*'s and out of love with worry.

When he realized that his son was broken, the phrase *damaged goods* played like a drum roll in his dreams. In some terrible way, Matt's midnight tape developed a second loop that replayed all of the moments he'd been a shitty father, impatient, grim-lipped when Collin snatched the newspaper out of his hands, whined at the store, messed his pants as they were about to go somewhere.

Some mornings he couldn't get out of bed. When he was on duty, he counted the minutes until he could get to Mickey's for a drink. The laughter, jokes, buddies who told him he was okay, made him believe it for a few hours. One night, drunk, he rubbed a hand on the uniformed back of a cheerful policewoman as she leaned toward him, listening to a joke someone was telling. Her skin was warm. So was his crotch. His hand drifted lower.

"Nice," he said. "I bet you wear a thong. You're that kind. Let's see it."

She pulled back, stepped down from the barstool. "You're an asshole."

He didn't remember the incident when the chief called him in, replayed it for him in the policewoman's words, told him she was considering filing harassment charges unless something was done to straighten him out. Captain McMillan said he understood what watching a kid's knees tremble then collapse, hearing a gurgle of a moan, feeling the weight of a warm gun in a hand, and knowing that an instant of fear and a tense finger had caused the pool of blood emptying out of a still body onto dark pavement, what that scene could do to a person. He added, "I also understand how a worrisome child can dismantle a marriage. I was in your shoes once, Matt." The captain seemed almost about to take his hand, then he sat back. "If I could do it, you can do it." He offered Matt a medical leave and a program for drying out, straightening out.

Matt hesitated, not sure he wanted to be straightened out, not sure he could be straightened out. Maybe, he said, he was just a failed cop and it was time to quit.

"Bullshit," Captain McMillan said, and he called in his secretary to begin the paperwork. Matt was relieved that someone had taken charge of his life, for a while at least.

Three months later, when Matt returned to the station, he found himself assigned to graffiti detail, a quiet re-entry into being a cop. At home, Madge and he settled into an uneasy compromise. He wouldn't drink, she wouldn't pull away when he touched her. For Collin's sake.

Then their pediatrician witnessed one of their son's intense meltdowns, learned that the boy had lost most of his words, communicated by waving his hands, watched the fingers tapping, tapping. He sent them to a specialist who diagnosed Collin as autistic on a midlevel, and added that because he was young, the boy might be able to overcome some of the condition's symptoms.

For the next two years, a therapist came to their home, worked with Collin, taught them both how to deal with him when she wasn't there. The tantrums reduced. He began to respond to questions, not with words so much as with gestures. He tried to look at them, as they asked him to, he frowning, turning away as if the effort were painful. He learned to say thank you when prompted.

They maintained some hope, mortgaging the house for a second time to pay for the therapy. Then came the weekend they had to accept the fact that their son would never be like other kids. Marge had put Collin to bed, the normal routine of three stories and a prayer. They had poured a glass of wine for Marge, a sparkling water for Matt, when Collin began to scream, piercing sounds that brought them to their feet. "Juicy Juice," he demanded, charging out of his room, stomping and flailing his pajama'd body at their feet.

"No sweets," Matt said.

"God, we have to do something." Marge reached for the juice carton.

"No, Marge." Matt grabbed her arm, and she spilled juice all over the counter and onto the floor.

"Juicy Juice!"

"Damn you, Matt."

Matt bent to pick up the boy, but the arms and legs interfered, caught him in the groin. Collin ran howling into his bedroom, then back out into the living room. He pounded on the front door, tried the knob.

"For God's sake, stop him, Matt."

"You stop him. I'm wiping up goddamn Juicy Juice." As he mopped the floor with a wad of paper towels, Matt wasn't sure at whom he was most angry, his son or his wife.

Collin managed that night to scream, cry, and run for three hours. When he finally fell into a deep sleep on the floor next to his bed, Matt and Marge, exhausted, stood looking down at their son.

"Not quite what we expected," Matt whispered.

Marge knew what he meant. "No," she answered as she turned away.

When he was five, they enrolled Collin in a special-ed classroom program, found a new medication, and tried a marriage counselor. Then they divorced, each of them exhausted.

Marge chose Paxil to get through her days; Matt had his work. They split the Collin duties, caring for him separately, inserting a cartilage of quiet hours between the days that rubbed bone on bone.

And now a year later, Marge is drained empty of love for her son. Matt can understand it. He himself can come up with only shadows when he thinks of Marge, and he is running low on love for his son. But not empty. Not yet. As he bends over his son, he hears the faint "Papa" as blue eyes close, lulled into sleep by a medicinal lullaby and chocolate milk, a scruffy gray rat tucked under a tender chin. No, not empty, just bewildered. How will he do this? A tightness grips his chest; he breathes five times through his nose.

Then he calls his mother.

CHAPTER FIVE

ELLIE

SEPTEMBER 2009

I am lying, of course, about the freesias. Maybe if she'd said nasturtiums, I wouldn't have had to. I haven't grown a flower since Danny was a first grader and he had a science project from school, a few white bean seeds. We dug some dirt from the edge of our apartment parking lot and we planted them in a plastic cup. Danny knew enough to punch a hole in the bottom for the water to drain out, and we set the cup on the windowsill over the sink. In a few days he came yelling to tell me that green was coming up.

A few weeks later we had real leaves and he took the cup to school for show-and-tell. He was so proud, walking stiff like a zombie, the cup protected under the corner of his jacket. When the teacher told him that the plants would need more room to grow, we put them in a coffee can, and by the time school was out, we had orange and yellow flowers trailing down the wall under the window and getting caught in the faucet handles.

I hand Sarah a tissue and she dabs and blows.

"Sorry," she says. "Sometimes I get weird." She blinks a few times. "My mother's dead," like that does it. "I guess I should go."

She looks up and down the street, and I can see gritty streaks on her neck. Kids' necks collect dirt like that. I feel like taking her home and scrubbing her with a soapy washrag even if she does yell. Well, maybe not. A person does that only to her own scrutty kid.

But she does need a shower and probably clean underwear. That seems reason enough for me to take her arm, turn her. "Come on home with me. You look hungry, and I know I am." She doesn't say anything, just follows me into the depressing building I've lived in for ten years, low income, low expectations. The elevator smells pissy, as usual, and I'm glad when we can get out. My apartment is three doors to the right, the one with the note taped on it. I rip it off since I know what it says. The rent is late again.

Everything is brown in this place. Seemed okay when I moved in and bought coordinated furnishings from Goodwill. Brown rug, brown davenport, brown fake-leather armchair. They matched the brown cabinets in the kitchen, the tan, going to brown, vinyl under them. Even a brown stove. Today, the air even seems brown, and I open a window, hoping to get a cool draft to cut into the unmoving heat of the radiator clicking against the wall. Brown was big, once.

"This is nice," Sarah says, dropping her bag at the door.

Now she's lying, but it shows some upbringing, just to say it. She waits until I take the collar of her jacket and pull her out of it. I wonder if duct tape washes. Also the flimsy top that barely covers her breasts and not her belly button. And that little rag of a skirt. If she bends over in it, anyone looking could see everything, but luckily instead, she sits down on the hassock and pulls her boots off, sparing me that. I point toward the armchair. She collapses into it, leans her head back, closes her eyes.

"While I'm heating up dinner," I say, "take advantage of my shower. Shampoo's there, and a towel. We'll eat and then relax. First things first."

She opens her eyes, and for a minute I think she's going to do that thing teenagers do with their mouths to let you know you're not thinking right, but then she shifts, and says, "Where's it at?" She's peeling off the blouse as she walks toward the bathroom, and I get a glimpse of a black ribbon of a bra as she opens the door. The sight makes me a little sad. My bras, black and otherwise, huddle at the bottom of a drawer, waiting, maybe, for a reason to wear them again.

Before she can get the water running, I call to her to throw out her clothes and I'll wash them in the basement laundry while we eat. When the clothes land in a heap in the hallway, I hand her the silk Japanese robe I've saved for a long time for some special occasion. Not that this is special, only unusual. And it won't wrap around me like it might have once. It will around her.

I think it's peculiar, looking into the cupboard over the stove, the fact that I have two boxes of mac and cheese and, in the fridge, a head of pretty good lettuce from the food bank I go to in between Social Security checks. But mostly, the fact that I have someone to eat it with. The last time I had a someone to dinner, he ate so fast, his dentures sliding in and out as he chewed, that he choked on a piece of canned ham, another gift of the food bank, and had to be carried out hyperventilating by the super who knew the Heimlich maneuver but not about panic attacks. Mr. Levitz was not much of a catch, I realized, way too old, and I ate the rest of the ham by myself.

I don't imagine this girl will choke on mac and cheese. And now I know what to do about it if she does. The water's still running, so I bundle up her clothes and take them down to the washers, grabbing the soap and the quarters from the jar as I go out.

By the time I get back, she's curling, legs up against her chest, into the chair, the robe wrapped around her. She looks new, red and orange and squeaky clean. She smiles at me from under a bow that holds her wet hair back, out of her eyes, just like her mother showed her, I bet, except the ribbon is the tie from the robe.

Ten minutes later we are sitting together on the davenport, eating out of our laps. She eyes the TV but doesn't ask.

"Don't have cable. I only get channels six and eight and twelve."

"I was on television once."

"Yeah?"

"Not my name, just me and some other kids. We were singing Christmas songs at Sunday school. My teacher said it was a way to say thank you to the people

who gave toys for foster kids who might not get any."
She closes up for a second, then looks at me. "I got a
jigsaw puzzle."

"I hate jigsaw puzzles."

"Me too." She pokes at her salad. "What's this?"

"Avocado. A little soft, but still good."

Sarah tastes a green slice. "Too gushy." Then her
face goes still again, her fork resting on the plate,
and I see the beginnings of tears. "I really wanted
Samantha Parkington. I put her on the wishing tree
at school and . . ." She wipes her wet cheek on the
sash which has dropped like a noose around her
neck, her hair falling back to her eyebrows. "I prayed
for her." Her eyes close, her salad forgotten. "I was
so stupid."

"You prayed for Samantha Parkington?"

"A beautiful doll I saw on TV. A real girl. I thought
she looked like me. Only she had brown eyes." Sarah
raises her head, finished with the tears. "I was just a
little kid then."

"Like four or so years ago?"

"Yeah." She sits up. "Sorry. I spilled." She scoops
up lettuce leaves with her fingers, places them back
on her plate, wipes off the pillow with her napkin.

"So, you were maybe eleven, you wanted this doll
who was a real girl with clothes and looked like you,

and you got a jigsaw puzzle?" I can't stand stories like this. If I could cry, I'd be wiping my eyes right now.

"That's about it." Sarah finishes the greens, gets up, her robe flapping open, her young breasts peeking out from under the forgotten sash like new white nasturtiums, and takes our dishes to the sink.

"Well, that sucks," I say. I'm not sure she hears me over the splashing of the water, the clanking of the pots. I go retrieve her clothes from the dryer.

"This was my grandmother's," I explain as I toss the quilt on the davenport. "Called Rose of Sharon. She made quilts in between kids." Sarah does not pick up on my need to talk a little. Her eyes close as soon as she pulls the quilt up over the T-shirt I've lent her. "Sleep tight," I say. I don't say the thing about bedbugs. She might think I'm serious.

She's left the towel on the floor and her bag in the sink. A flash of *oh, shit* passes through me as I pick up the towel, fold it and hang it on the bar. I don't need this aggravation. *It's only for one night,* I remind myself.

The duffel is gaping open and a wet toothbrush is lying beside the faucet. I am wondering if I should put it in the glass next to mine or mind my own business and just push the whole thing under the sink, when I see the cigarettes. What else? Underpants, a beat-up address book, a few wadded-up clothes, a plastic bag stuffed with makeup, a pill container, and a condom. Traveling supplies, I guess. I take out the plastic vial. Its label has been mostly peeled off; brown pills rattle inside. I put it back.

Not my business. She'll leave in the morning. I push the duffel under the sink, wash my face, and smooth a couple of dots of Pond's on my cheeks. I do this every night. My fingers, pressing lightly on my cheeks and temples, soothe me. I remember other fingers doing the same when this face did not need a cream to make it touchable, and most of the time, I sleep better thinking about them.

I wake up wondering where she keeps her monthly supplies if not in her bag. Then I hear why I woke up. Someone's throwing up in the bathroom. She comes out rubbing her mouth on the T-shirt, pale and watery-eyed. "Must have a bug," she says.

"Then you won't need breakfast," I answer, putting my two wonderings together, pissed at her lying. So easy to get sucked in, I remind myself. Not my problem. "Coffee, maybe." I put on the water and begin to figure out what I'm going to say to her as I measure out a couple of teaspoons of instant. "Listen, Missy," I'll say. "I got no time for girls who mess around, get pregnant, run away, end up with duct-taped jackets. Mother or no mother, you have a family somewhere to handle this mess. A bit late for the condom, don't you think? And what the hell are you doing with those ugly brown pills?" By the time the water is steaming, so am I.

I turn around to hand her the cup and my words, and she is gone. All of her, even the bag from the bathroom and the pile of clean clothes, I see when I go look for her.

Not even a thank-you. I fold up the Rose of Sharon quilt and sit down next to it on the davenport with my coffee.

I never learned to make quilts even though my grandmother encouraged me to try. Once, she even made a little sewing kit and cut out squares of printed cotton and brought them to me as I loafed on my bed, reading a comic book. She held out her offerings, sat down and prodded me until I threaded the needle and sewed two squares together. Then I said, "That's it, Ma" and got up and dropped needles and thread, the fabric, and my teenage disgust in her lap. Not even a thank-you.

Remembering like that isn't good for a person. I glance at the clock. Almost noon; time for my daily dose of Perry Mason. Perry never has doubts or bad memories to screw up his day. While I'm watching him, I don't either.

CHAPTER Six

SARAH

September 2009

It's lucky the park is only a couple of blocks away. I'm going to barf again. I can feel it clogging my throat, my mouth watering. I'm not going to make it to the john. I head for the bushes at the edge of the walkway, lean in, let go. I'm hanging onto a branch, sweating and shaking when I feel a hand on my elbow.

"Take it easy, girl. Let's go sit down."

My eyes are too bleary to see who is leading me or to where. When I stumble, an arm reaches around my waist then releases me to a seat on a wooden bench. He sinks down next to me and wipes my mouth with something, my jacket collar probably. His voice is jagged, the way old smokers sound. His beard, once I can see his face, confirms my guess. It's white with black streaks, nicotine yellow at the edges.

"You're hot," he says. "You got something." He pulls a bundle from his pocket, a bottle in a paper sack, is about to hand it to me, then takes a swallow himself. "You don't want this. Even makes me sick. Stay here and I'll get you some water."

His long overcoat flaps against his ankles as he shuffles toward the fountain. In a moment he's back, a plastic bag spurting water in his hands. I manage to get a mouthful, then dash a little against my face. The cold feels good on my cheeks. I really am hot. "Thanks," I say. I'm not sure I can stand up.

"Where do you live? Around here?"

"I'm okay. Just have to rest for a minute." He hesitates and then gets up. "I have an appointment," he says. "I'll be back."

"Sure." His appointment is with a bottle. I'm too tired to think of what to do next. I close my eyes.

I wake up when the bench shakes and someone sits next to me, breathing hard.

"Sorry. I had to get my teeth cleaned. Are you feeling better?"

"Teeth cleaned?"

He grins. His teeth are white, healthy-looking, except for the one in front that is missing. So are his brown eyes. They smile at me. "At the Williams House. Every week the medical bus comes and treats people. For nothing. If you make an appointment, you can get your teeth cleaned."

"Not my teeth that's bothering me." Maybe I ate something bad last night—the avocado? I'm still sick to my stomach. "Thanks for helping me. I'm okay."

"Rick. I'm Rick."

I don't want to give him my name. You have to be careful. Made that mistake with the old lady, who seemed okay until she went through my bag, looking for who knows what. She knew I didn't have any money—maybe my address or something that could identify me. None of her business. Or anybody's. "I'll be going," I say, and before I can stand up, I throw up again, between my legs, splashing Rick's dusty shoe. "Guess not."

"Come on," he says, taking hold of my arm. "I'll bring you to the nurse. She can give you something." He picks up my bag and pulls me up. "Only a block or so."

A big white bus is parked in a lot next to a church. People are lined up at the door, but Rick goes right past them and says, "This little lady needs a doctor right now," as he pushes me up the stairs. "Upchucking," he explains, and I must look like I'm about to do it again because a woman watching us finds a bag before she leads me to a chair.

"Eating all right?" she asks as she sticks a plastic tape in my mouth. "Under your tongue. Or something else?" In a moment she takes the tape out of my mouth and says, "Oh, oh. Something else." Her fingers hold my wrist as she looks at her watch, and then she says, "Oh, oh" again when she sees the goosebumps on my arm. "Chilly?" she asks.

I nod and sink back into the chair. "I don't feel good. My chest hurts so much I can hardly breathe."

"Tired, too, I bet."

I close my eyes for a minute.

"You probably have the flu," she says, as she waves a wooden stick in front of my mouth and signals for me to open up. "We'll take a culture to make sure. In the meantime, you need to go to bed."

I'd tell her that I don't have a bed, but I begin to cough so hard I almost vomit again.

"Lots of liquids, clear soup, Tylenol, and here's a sample of cough syrup that may help." She takes a paper from her desk. "For our records, for when you come back, your name, address, age?" Then she asks, "Might you be pregnant? That might change things."

I get up and make my way to the door. "No name, no address," I croak. I wave her away and step carefully down the steps. "I'm just glad it isn't something serious." Then I faint into Rick's body and wake up lying on a cot in the back of the bus, the woman leaning over me. "We'll get you to the teen shelter. They can give you a bed."

I manage to raise my head and say, "No." I wonder if I can sit up.

I won't go back to that place with its losers bellyaching about how hot it is sitting on sidewalks with their dogs, how people say shitty things to them, how all they need was a fuckin' hand up, while their own hands are busy rolling smokes, hiding bottles, popping pills. No, anything will be better than that, even the old lady's brown apartment. I sit up, tell the woman that I have a place just down the block, my grandma's, and drag my bag down the steps before someone tries to stop me.

If anyone asks, I can't remember my grandma's name.

Ellie, it's Ellie. That's the only buzzer that seems to make sense, on the third floor. I push it. Again. A voice, familiar, says, "If you're selling something, go away."

"It's me. Sarah. I need help. I'm sick." As if to prove the truth in my claim, I lean over the porch's iron railing and throw up into a rhododendron. The lock clicks. I wipe my mouth on my sleeve, open the door, and head toward the elevator. When I get out on the third floor, Ellie is standing, hands on hips, in the middle of the hallway.

"So you've decided to come back," she says, but whatever else she means to say is interrupted when I fall onto her body, my arms around her neck.

"I'm really sick," I mumble into her shoulder, and I feel myself being dragged into the apartment and laid out on the davenport.

Ellie yanks off my stockings and boots, spreads a quilt across my legs. Cool cloths wrap my forehead. A bucket waits on the floor if I should need to throw up again—just the way a grandma would do it. Then I go to sleep, and when I wake up the room is gray with morning. Ellie is sleeping in the big chair across the room, her fuzzy white hair glowing a little in the morning light, her mouth open, soft sounds wheezing out, her wrinkled hands, like soft armor, spread across her breasts.

I have been here before, I realize, not here, but in this same moment, a sleeping woman keeping watch as I wake up, terrified, but safe. I am five, maybe, and breathing fast from a nightmare, the kind that has fractured my sleep ever since my father left us. The woman is my mother, the mother I remember with love, the mother who doesn't kill herself for another three years. I close my eyes.

CHAPTER SEVEN

JEFF

1993-1996

The afternoon Jeff and Danny skip a sixth grade science test and go boarding at the skate park under the freeway, they end up resting against a pillar, drinking the beer that Danny has taken from his mother's fridge. Trucks and cars roar above their heads, thunder across the spacers, the sounds vibrating all through Jeff's body. Moving his arms to the rhythm of the traffic overhead, he spills some beer on Danny's pants. He leans over and uses his jacket sleeve to wipe it off.

"Hey, fag, cut it out." Danny pushes his arm away.

"I'm not a fag, fag. What's your problem?" Jeff pretends to be mad, but the way Danny grins and turns the can up to his mouth again gives Jeff a jolt of courage. "Have you ever done it? You know." He thrusts his hips forward and back to demonstrate what he means.

Danny shrugs. "Almost, with Ginny." He is lying, Jeff can tell by the way his friend is looking down into his beer.

"I mean . . . " Jeff reaches his hand out, his palm hovers over Danny's zipper, his fingers forming a circle, and he makes Grandpa Jack's night sounds.

Danny jerks away from him. "What the fuck?"

Jeff laughs like he's been joking.

"I gotta go," Danny says as he stands up and tosses the can into the gutter. A moment later he is pushing up the street, popping over curbs, sending a *see ya* wave over his shoulder to Jeff, who leans back against the concrete and finishes his beer.

A scroungy cat sidles up to him, mewing at his empty can, and he plays with it for a few minutes, dragging the pulltab across its paws. Then, bored or maybe sad—Jeff doesn't have a name for the feeling that wanders through him pretty much most of the time—he flips his Bic and holds the flame to the tip of the cat's tail. It bolts off down the street, trailing smoke and peals of screams behind it, and Jeff, smiling despite his bad mood, wonders what Danny is doing. Not lighting cats on fire, that's for sure. Danny likes animals.

By the time they get to high school, Danny's mother is supplying their booze, the fridge always stocked with Pabst, the cupboard above it with her whiskey of choice, Southern Comfort usually. Jeff has made connections in the drug world, deals a little, and during their junior year, they spend half their days on Ellie's davenport, trying to focus on her rolling TV screen. "This is child abuse," Jeff complains more than once. "She's got to get a new TV if she thinks we're going to stick around."

Danny laughs, pulls out another beer. "At least the fridge works."

For the past eight years, Jeff's grandfather has taken his parenting responsibilities seriously, lecturing his grandson regularly on the value of study and excellent English and good manners. He sticks notes, vocabulary words neatly printed on them, on the cupboards and mirrors. "To nudge the subconscious," he tells his grandson. "Another way to attain knowledge." Jeff is pretty sure the stickies don't work, and he is sick of the lectures, the words, and his grandfather. He begins, at sixteen, to turn him off, muttering "fuck it," often leaving the old man in midsentence in front of a slammed front door.

And much of the time, Jeff also manages to avoid Grandpa Jack's bedtime visits by staying over at Danny's or by passing out as soon as he hits the pillow.

After a while, his grandfather seems to avoid him in return. Some days he doesn't do more than glance at Jeff over his morning coffee, the one time of day they cross paths. When he thinks about it, Jeff realizes this coldness started the night Jeff laughed at the old man's lifeless penis and rolled away, pulling the blankets after him. Grandpa Jack gasped, pretended he had a cough, and said, "Good night." The mattress creaked as he stood up. Still grinning, Jeff whispered, "Good-bye, old man," into his pillow.

One Saturday morning, having just opened the front door feeling like roadkill, he finds his grandfather's pointed, shaking finger greeting him.

"Déjà vu, Jeff. This is your father all over again. After all I've done for you."

Jeff pushes into the room. He hates the way his grandfather's jowls tremble when his mouth moves. "Yeah, whatever."

"Even the way you've reverted to sloppy low-class language. What happened to our one-new-word-a-day plan? And to the idea that speaking well is the key to success in life?"

Jeff pours himself a glass of orange juice to calm his stomach. He chugs it, reaches for more. "I remember *innocuous*. It's kind of the way you're acting now." He pours, drinks, puts the glass down, and faces his grandfather. "*Insipid*, right? God, nobody I know uses fucking words like that. So I'm *recalcitrant*?"

During their first years of sitting at the breakfast table together, Grandpa Jack fed him words like that, and Jeff swallowed them like the cereal in the bowl in front of him. He even used a few of them until the other kids started laughing at him.

"Even so, Jeff, later you'll need a good vocabulary, just as I have."

His grandfather's hair is thin now, oiled streaks threaded across his scalp, his eyebrows white, one always sprouting a long hair that flutters over the metal frame of his glasses. His belt rides low under a belly, his trousers wrinkled and empty.

"Old man, you and I are living on the foster care check you get every month for taking me in. And I've never understood the workman's comp checks that keep coming for no good reason. What success are you talking about?"

"I'm thinking of you. Of you as a man of the world."

Jeff swallows against the suddenly bitter liquid clogging his throat. "You have never thought of me as a man." As the words squeeze out, Jeff also understands a truth about himself. Neither has he. The edges of his eyelids burn. He resists rubbing them.

His grandfather's freckled hand reaches toward him. "We have something special, Jeff."

Jeff's fist swings at the hand, grazes it. "Special? You used me." He hasn't cried in years, but tears blur his grandfather's face. He steps closer, tall enough now to look down at the old man, the words breaking through, a flood. "I don't know what the hell I am, not a man of the world, for God's sake. I'm a collection of body parts, a useful ass, a talented tongue, a *solipsist*—isn't that the word? —for your special needs."

Jeff understands something else at this moment. He wipes his cheek on his collar, tears extinguished in a cry of disgust. "Shit. My father, Bucky, too, right?" He turns, looks for his jacket. "I'm following him right out of here. I don't need you anymore."

"*Solecism*, Jeff. But you mean *solace*. You should be careful with words. They do make a difference." His grandfather stops talking, removes his glasses, squints at the lens. "You are referring to drug money, I assume."

"And other money. You taught me well, Grandpa Jack. I suppose I should thank you."

As Jeff heads to his room for the last time, Grandpa Jack is waving a hand in front of his left eye. Something appears to be annoying him.

CHAPTER EIGHT

MATT

2000

Grace answers the phone with her usual hesitancy. Her "hello" is followed by a question mark. When she hears his voice, another question: "Matt?" It has been weeks since she's heard from him, the last conversation ending abruptly when a call came in on his radio. Then, "What's wrong?"

Something often has been wrong in the past when he's called his mother, like the time he informed her that he had gotten married to Marge over the weekend because she was pregnant—not that that was wrong, but it wasn't the way he knew Grace had wanted it to happen. Or the call from the clinic to let her know he wouldn't be around for a month or three until he got through the rehab. Or, perhaps the worst call of all, the one telling her of the doctor's diagnosis of her grandson's strange behavior.

And later, the call in which she learned of her son's divorce. Matt can't remember when he's called to tell her good news.

His mother has always taken bad news with a stoicism that he used to believe made her a compliant sponge, especially when it came to his father, especially the times her cheek had been reddened by his hand, and she had turned away from the drunk-angry man to stir whatever was on the stove. When her husband died, killed in an automobile crash, Grace shed fifteen minutes of tears and then, chin raised, took over the raising of her two children, Matt and his sister, Patty.

Their life as a family continued as it had been before his father's death, except that they were poorer and Grace worked long hours. He and his sister followed their usual separate paths, he continuing to be the good child and Patty enjoying the role of the wild child early on. By high school, she was doing things Matt hadn't even thought of, even though he was two years older. "God, Patty, be careful," he'd say, and she'd laugh, pull a condom out of her purse or a baggie of marijuana or some other souvenir of the weekend, and call him a pussy. Then she'd hug him, say something like, "It's okay, bro. I know what I'm doing." He wanted to believe her.

One night a policeman knocked on the door. He told them that a girl, believed to be Patty Trommald, had died from an overdose in a park on the other side of town. Could a family member come with him, perhaps identify her? Grace sent Matt to make sure the dead girl was some druggie from somewhere else, not his sister. "It couldn't be Patty. God wouldn't let this happen to our sweet girl, would she?" she asked, heart-stoppingly hopeful.

Matt found Patty lying in a grassy field, surrounded by cops and onlookers. Blue-lipped and staring, in death his sister was still beautiful. As he held her cold hand, he understood that if he had been a better brother he could have stopped her from using. He should have listened harder, maybe told his mother, asked someone at school for advice. But he hadn't.

When he reported back to Grace, his mother wept, clung to him as he held her, himself in tears, both of them taking blame for Patty's death. In the months that followed, Matt buried his feelings in schoolwork and Grace continued to weep when she looked into photo albums. Patty, a scrunch-face newborn in the first book; Patty, her dark eyes bright and expectant, on the arm of her first prom date, just months ago.

One day Grace closed the album in her lap and said, "It's up to you, Matt, from now on." Matt wasn't sure what the "it" was. Grow up, probably. He could do that. He went to community college for a couple of years, worked as a security guard to bring money home. He was accepted to the police academy and a little later, got married like a responsible adult. He hoped that's what his mother meant about "it," living a normal life, having a family, calling her once in a while with his news.

"Please don't call unless it's good news, Matt," his mother asked after the divorce. "I'm getting too old for this."

And so he did as she asked, until now.

"What's wrong?"

"I need your help, Grace. Marge has given Collin to me." His throat closes. "For good." He wonders if he can get any more words out.

"I see." His mother hesitates no longer than a breath. "I'll be there tomorrow morning."

The radio message comes in a few minutes before he is due to take the squad car back to the pound and retrieve his own car to pick up Collin from his school. He phones his mother to say they'll be a little late, not to worry.

"Spaghetti tonight," she answers. "I'll pick him up if I need to."

She's probably relieved that she can see the end of *Dr. Phil.* Collin doesn't like *Dr. Phil.* Other than that, it's worked out pretty well these past months. Collin, almost eight, has words now, a few. Just enough to calm the frustration he shows when no one understands what he needs or wants. He likes to be read to. He plays a kind of game only he understands, a repetitive placing of checkers on a board, while Grandma Grace watches and cheers him on. She has a gentle, mostly silent relationship with him, reading his gestures almost as well as his occasional words. She knows when to touch him, when not to.

"You were born to be Collin's grandmother," Matt tells her one afternoon when he comes home to find them sitting cross-legged in the middle of the living room floor, seriously building towers of dominoes.

And perhaps he was born to be Collin's father, he thinks a day or so later, when Collin reaches for his hand for the first time as they walk to the ice cream shop a few blocks away.

Matt stops in front of the low-income apartment house the call has come from. Fourth floor, 416; a female says her son is the mugger the newspaper wrote about that day, the one where the victim died from a heart attack an hour after he was robbed. No elevator. He's breathing hard by the time he knocks on the door, which opens quickly, a woman clutching the frame, drops of blood on her blouse. She smells of whiskey.

"Sergeant Trommald. May I come in?"

The door opens a bit more; the woman steps back. Her left arm is wrapped around her ribs, and she stumbles as she steps back. "We don't need you anymore. It's all settled."

Matt can imagine how the problem, whatever it is, has been settled. He checks his note. "Mrs. Miller. You called about your son. Is he here?" A head pokes out from behind an open door.

"Come on out," Matt calls. He is relieved when the kid steps into the room, nothing in his hands, and hesitates a few feet away.

"You said your son was involved in a robbery. Is this him?" At her nod, Matt pats the boy down—nothing but a can of chew.

"Yes, but it was a mistake." The fumes from her breath seep into the stale fog of the room, and

Matt looks around. The table holds an empty bourbon bottle, a smudged glass, half a bag of Cheetos. "Danny? That right? The report named a Danny. What do you know about this?" he asks the boy.

Danny seems sober, even close to tears. "She's nuts." When he starts to turn away, Matt puts his hand out and stops him.

The woman, hard to tell how old she is—fifty-something, maybe, but alcohol and the mess of graying hair may have added a few years—looks about to crumple to the floor. She straightens, lifts her chin, and says, carefully, in control of her words, "It is my fault. I was angry with Danny because the school reported him absent again, and I decided to call the station and say he might have done something bad, to scare him. I'm so afraid that he'll really go wrong, do something even worse than mugging someone, something that will send him to prison and ruin his life. He's a good boy, but he was mad when he heard me call. We ended up hitting each other, but we're over it, aren't we, Danny?"

Danny doesn't look at either of them. "Sure, whatever," he mutters. This time Matt steps aside, lets the kid go back to the room he's come out of.

"I lied." The woman's still holding her ribs. "On the phone. Danny was here all yesterday."

Matt shrugs, disgusted. He has enough time to pick up Collin if he hurries. "Family disturbance? Is that correct?" He jots a note in his pad, steps to the door. "Don't let it happen again, Mrs. Miller. Next time he might do some real harm."

It isn't until he's halfway down the stairs that he remembers he's met this woman before. When he was in the graffiti office, he was sent to calm down a woman who claimed she was the only person in her end of town doing anything about the graffiti slathered on the mailboxes and street signs.

"Not only that," she complained, her frowzy hair waving at him, "it is costing me money, and the stuff the hardware store is selling me is no good. Seems like someone in city hall could lend a hand." Matt, newly versed in graffiti problems, put her on the list to receive Graffiti X regularly. She wasn't drunk that time, but he does remember, now that he thinks about it, the acrid scent of pot that hit him when he came through the door. Probably the kid in the back room. Danny.

Maybe he should have intervened. Like maybe someone should have intervened twenty years ago when a drunk father created havoc for a couple of kids, and his mother wrapped her soft presence around them to protect them. Probably not. Nothing changes until the time is right, or never.

Matt gets to the school in time to lead Collin to his car, as usual. Collin hates to have his routine messed up.

CHAPTER NINE

ELLIE

SEPTEMBER 2009

Friday is my day to go to the food bank, and if I'm going to have someone living with me for a few days, I have to go out, sick or not. Actually, the girl seems better after a night's sleep, not eating anything much, but she's propped up and looking at herself in the mirror she's found in her duffel. She apparently doesn't like what she sees, because she's still rummaging around and pulling out the plastic bag holding her makeup.

"No eye makeup," I say. "You look like a corpse in that black stuff, and you look bad enough without it."

"Just a little blush," she says. She is pretty, in a skinny sort of way, her hair straight as a stick and black, but brown near the part. If she lets it grow out a little, she'll look like a calico cat, orange and black, a look that will suit the way she's stretching right now, lying back against the pillow.

"I'll be gone for a while. Depends on when the buses come and how long the lines are at the food place. Anything special you want me to look for? Not that I'll find it, but sometimes you get lucky. Last week they had cherries that farmers couldn't sell because they had a bumper crop. And one time we got canned hams." I won't tell her that story now, but later it might get her to laugh a little. "I don't understand where the hams came from—some ham bumper crop, I suppose." She wiggles a good-bye finger at my little joke.

I liked last night, the waiting and watching. I used to be good at it. Back when. Back before. The bus pulls in, and I am too busy trying to find a dollar in change and counting pennies to keep that thought going.

When I get home a couple of hours later, Sarah greets me with wet hair tucked behind her ears and wearing the red silk robe. She has hot water ready for coffee. We unload my bags and I show her the prize of the day, a bottle of almost-maple syrup. Eggs, too. We'll have French toast for dinner, if she feels like eating. I hope she does.

I notice that she has rearranged a few things. A book I had forgotten I had is open on the end table.

The table lamp is moved toward her end of the davenport. The picture frame under it is crooked, as if she's been studying the face it holds. She sees me noticing. "I got bored. I guess I'm getting better."

I straighten the photo, and she says, "He's cute. Is he around?"

"No," I say, and I go to the kitchen and fold the paper bags for recycling.

We spend the rest of the day without talking much, me watching Channel 12 and Sarah looking for a lost earring and then reading the book she turned up instead, a mystery I got for twenty-five cents at Goodwill a while back. I can trade two paperbacks in for an unread one at Mary's Second Glance bookstore, and I'm glad Sarah found this one under the davenport. If there is another book under there, I'll go back to Mary's tomorrow. I'd like Sarah to take a look, but she's deep into Sue Grafton and I don't want to disturb her. I know how that feels, to be carried away.

By the weekend, Sarah's up and I'm wondering when she will take off again. By now she's calling me Ellie and I kind of like it, but I know she can't like living in a dingy apartment with an old lady who gets crabby when she can't find a paperback mystery or when the cherries turn out to be wormy. She has told me about the man who helped her at the medical bus, and from her description, I know she's talking about Rick, who lives in a small room in the basement of this building and keeps his grocery cart under the stairs.

He's a nice guy when he's on his meds, and he usually is. Once in a while, I'll hear him pushing his cart down the middle of the street, arguing with invisible nurses at the VA or yelling about the unfairness of the postal service or whining about being abandoned by a girl, a beautiful girl, at his senior prom, his life not the same since. But usually, he's fine, and once a week he goes through the recycling bins in the neighborhood and picks up pocket money from the bottles he finds there. He offered me a piece of dark chocolate with hazelnuts from Trader Joe's on one of those days.

I can imagine him helping Sarah, and I say sure when she asks if she could thank him with a plate of French toast.

Sarah comes back with a square of chocolate. "I gave him my earring, too, the mate to the silver star one that I lost, because I remembered the empty hole in his ear. He liked it, he said."

I'm a little jealous. Young people make friends so easy. Danny could, too, ten years ago, only what he was trading came in crystals and capsules, rustling plastic bags. He had lots of friends. I didn't suspect a thing. I'm smarter now.

That's why I think she's lying when she answers my question about leaving by saying she has no place to go, that she doesn't like the people in the shelters.

She left one shelter and tried to live on her own, she says, but it didn't work out. "Then I met some people living in the forest above the park. They invited me to join their camp, and for a while, it was okay. Seven or eight of us, three girls, the rest guys, lived there. We ate whatever we found in garbage bins in back of restaurants, and we had a campfire every night and told stories. About our lives and stuff. I thought it was kind of fun."

Sarah stops for a moment, a cloud of a frown passing across her eyebrows. "Starkey called us his family. He said he was like a father because he was older and could take care of us. He told us not to be afraid, we'd all look out for each other, but we had to do what he said, or he might have to punish us. Like a father would. Sometimes, to prove our loyalty to the family, he told us we had to steal something, like beer or Twinkies, or to—you won't like this, Ellie—to leave messages on buildings or other places so other people would know we were in the neighborhood."

"On mailboxes?"

Sarah nods, shrugs like she's embarrassed. "But my main job was to collect firewood and to help clean up the camp. And I Dumpster-dived because I was small and could be lifted right into the bin. I made a friend or two, and I felt safe, you know, like somebody cared about me." She looks at me to see if I understand.

"You left Starkey and your friends because?"

"I stopped feeling safe."

I don't want to hear anymore. I'm surprised at how disappointed I am about guessing right about Sarah and the graffiti. Who knows, maybe about her being pregnant, too. I don't even want to think about the flower tattoo. Or the brown pills. So I change the subject. "We're taking another tour of the mailboxes even though tomorrow is only Tuesday. You owe me. Room and board."

And I decide that by Wednesday she'll have to find another family to be safe in. I'm not that family. I'm not good at it.

CHAPTER TEN

SARAH

SEPTEMBER 2009

We're walking toward the first mailbox, Ellie frowning and looking at my arm as if she wants to touch it. I can understand that. I like to, too; the pink and fuchsia and purple blossoms feel warm and soft under my fingertips.

My mother had soft cheeks. I remember my lips kissing them good night, my fingers reaching to pat them as she read to me. She was soft all over, especially her chest with its pillows that my head fit between. Now that I'm older I realize she was probably pretty fat, but little kids don't notice stuff like that when they are five, which is as far back as I can go. I was sad then, crying a lot, needing to be held.

Or maybe it was my mother who was sad. Maybe I held her, the two of us crying into each other. My father had left us, gone even to his scruffy bedroom slippers in the bottom of the closet, even to his tooth-brush except for its soapy outline against the sink's edge. He may have told her why he was leaving, but my mother didn't talk about it. We got through the worst part of being abandoned with me on her lap as she read to me.

Then I started a new school and met some friends and a teacher I liked. I still had my mother, and my mother had her job at the laundry and her garden on the south side of our rental house, where she grew tomatoes and cut bouquets of flowers that she put in glass vases in all our rooms and on the porches of a few of the neighbors. Tulips and daf-fodils in the spring, lilies and daisies in the summer, asters and chrysanthemums in the fall. She said she loved the freesias most of all because they were ten-der and needed loving care, had to grow on the protected side porch where she could sit after work on cool spring evenings and watch their buds open. Sometimes I would sit beside her, and we would tell stories, me the first sentence, her the second, until one of us fell asleep.

My mother also had her tall yellow drink, rattling with ice cubes every evening.

How could a little kid know how sad her mother was?

She died when I was eight. Someday maybe I'll understand why, but on the evening she took the brown pills that killed her, my mother sent me to a neighbor, saying that she was not feeling well; could she watch me for a while? The note I found on the kitchen table told me that she loved me, and I still believe her even though the foster homes I went to over the next seven years made me wonder why she would leave me to strangers. A hand under my nightgown in the last one sent me packing in the middle of the night. If I had to live with strangers, I'd choose them, I told myself.

I felt very brave that morning as I got on the light rail and headed toward downtown, my bag over my shoulder. I wondered if the woman with the shopping cart sitting next to me could tell I was running away. I smiled at her, but she didn't smile back. I might have frightened her. I looked like a street kid with my duffel and the boots I stole from my foster mother's closet. *Well*, I thought, *get used to it. I am a street kid.*

At first I stayed at a teen shelter where I got food and met a woman who encouraged me to make some decisions, go back to school, get involved in activities, find a better place to live. I hated most of the kids who ate and slept there, although I liked her, but going to an art class or writing in a journal didn't make me feel better about my life or myself.

I was still an orphan. I still missed my mother. I still wondered why she left me. The best I could do to bring her back was to go with a sort-of friend from the shelter to his buddy Ben's apartment in China-town and have Ben tattoo my arm with the freesia copied from the picture I tore out of a book in the library. All Ben would charge me was a blow job after every session. I guess he realized I was jailbait and didn't ask for anything more. It seemed like a good deal, and when it was finished, Ben said it was the best piece of art he'd ever done. He took a picture of it the last time I saw him, after I made my final payment.

I got sick of the shelter after a couple of months—the earnest volunteers, the kids taking advantage of them, the stories they bragged about when adults weren't listening. One night I just left. I walked around downtown, met a girl with a back-pack and a dog, and shared some stale cinnamon rolls and a joint. Then I curled up in a blanket in a doorway, my duffel under my head, the dog at my feet, the girl a little older than me, huddled next to me.

I can do this, I thought. *For as long as I have to.* The concrete was hard, and its cold crept into my bones, but I covered my head and had just about fallen asleep when I heard them. Three guys, laughing, standing over us, shadows against the streetlight.

"Sluts."

"Need to be taught a lesson."

"They probably know all the lessons." More laughing. The dog growled, rolled over, still asleep. I felt something poke at me, my shoulder, my stomach. "Wake up, little pussy. Company."

"Fuck off," I answered, trying to sound tough.

"That's what we've got in mind," one of them said.

"Smiley, what's happening?" Smiley was the street name I had decided on when my new friend told me I shouldn't use my real name if I was escaping from something. Hers was Fingers. She was good with them, she said, in 7-Eleven's candy and peanut butter aisles. "What's happening?"

I still needed to be tough, so I said, "These shits think we've got something they want."

Fingers sat up and reached for her dog. "One word and you're his dinner." The dog blinked, laid his head back down. The guys laughed, and one put his hand on Fingers' breast. She swung at him and he caught her arm, pulled her up to standing. The other two moved in on me. One of them leaned down and breathed on my face. I could smell sour beer. "We could take them right here," he said. His hand wandered over my body, landed on my hip, pressed against me. I wanted to scream, but other hands held me by my hair and throat, and all I could do was croak. I could hear Fingers swearing and saw the blackness of two bodies moving against the wall next to me.

"Come on," I heard him say. "Get it wet, darlin.' I'm coming in."

Fingers' "Like hell you . . . " was ended by the *thunk* of something hard against something hollow.

"What the fuck." The hand wrapped around my throat and hair loosened. The fingers poking at my body pulled away. I opened my eyes and saw punching arms, kicking legs, and flying bats. Fingers crouched at my side, the two of us watching the three thugs getting the shit kicked out of them.

When it was all over, Fingers wasn't crying like I was. She just rolled up her stuff and said thank you to the batboys. "Take it easy, Smiley," she said to me. "I'm out of here." And she turned and walked up the street, the dog following at her side.

Peter and Jimmy, their names were. Peter was tall and looked a little like Jake Gyllenhaal. Jimmy was round and sweaty. They were out patrolling, looking for lowlifes, they said.

"You found them," I answered. "Do I qualify as a low-life?" I meant the fact that I was sleeping in a doorway and had a name like Smiley and smelled like the pot I'd shared with Fingers.

They helped me pick up my stuff and said they had a safe place for a girl like me, who would never be considered a lowlife no matter where she slept.

I stop remembering stuff like this when I see the shoe in the leaves.

CHAPTER ELEVEN

ELLIE

SEPTEMBER 2009

The girl's hiccupping sobs keep me moving fast, past Rick's cart, down the hall, into the elevator, which for once is waiting for us. As the doors close, I punch the button and whisper, "Hold on and be quiet," to a frightening slough-off of mascara. All the doors on my floor will be flinging open if she keeps up the noise. My neighbors love any distraction in their Meals On Wheels lives.

I have my keys out of my pocket and into the locks just as her loudest wail flings itself down the hall. "Oh, God, I shouldn't have left Peter there with those people." Actually, there were no people, just a lot of leaves, I want to say, but I open the door instead. "Go wash your face while I phone." I point to the bathroom door.

When Sarah comes back to the door, smudged but not hiccupping anymore, I have finished the call. "No, I don't want to give you my name," I say, as I hang up. I suppose they can trace the call, but since the phone is out in the hallway, there are twenty suspects. None of their business who I am.

And Sarah is none of my business from this moment on. Not after seeing the shoe, remembering how ten years ago, as I curled up on the kitchen floor, my eighteen-year-old son aimed a similar Nike at my stomach, yelling that he wished I was dead. Haven't had to think of that night for a long time until now, until Sarah. This boy isn't Danny. I could see that as soon as his young face gazed out at the sky. My son would not be young anymore. He might be under a pile of leaves, though, somewhere. Who knows?

"Are the police coming?"

"Not here. To the street. He'll be gone in a minute."

"I don't want to go out until . . . " The girl can't seem to light anywhere, wandering from one spot to another, looking into a cupboard, touching a table-top, and then picking up the picture frame, looking at a kid who had slicked back his long hair into a pompadour. "Who'd you say this is?"

"None of your business," I say. A siren blares frantic bleeps a block away and then is silent. "And that dead person who is being carted away as we speak is none of my business either, even though it is apparent that you know him." I grab the picture from her and put it back on the table. "I don't want to hear about it, and I want you to leave before I get sucked into the kind of trouble I've managed to avoid for years. I don't do police. I don't do murders. I don't do homeless girls who would not be homeless if they had any sense."

"I might be pregnant."

"I couldn't care less."

Actually, I do care. The shock of that shoe poking out of the leaves has me wallowing in memories I thought I'd buried away for good. Me, pregnant, crazy in love with a fool who left me as soon as I miscarried. My grandmother washed her hands of me, and I spent the next twenty years wandering from bed to bed, one or two of them my own during the times I quit drinking and got a grip on life. I was living in an apartment when I brought someone home from a tavern to help me celebrate my thirty-seventh birthday. My birthday present to myself was a unmemorable roll in the hay, an ivory-handled knife that had slipped between the cushions of the couch we had wrestled on, and fifteen years wiping a snotty nose, combing for lice, waiting for the school to call, and chaining myself to a job in a cannery. I ended up with food on our table most of the time, a few good laughs, and varicose veins. When Danny asked, I couldn't remember his father's name, only that the guy stole my last pack of cigarettes as he snuck out the door sometime early that morning. I didn't mention that I wasn't sure which had made me madder, the ciggies or the sneaking. I did tell Danny that he was the best birthday surprise ever, no matter what. I'm not sure he believed me. He and I were not percolating much trust by then.

Finally, being a mother didn't work for me anymore. I wasn't up to it. I look at Sarah, and even though I am angry at her for trying to get into my life, I can't wish my story on her. And I can't watch it repeat from the sidelines, either. "You are out of here tomorrow."

The next morning, the door slams and I mutter, "Good riddance." One sleepless night has convinced me I am right. Maybe pregnant. Crying for hours about her Peter under the leaves and about a camp in the forest where she'd gotten to know him. She shouldn't have left the camp, she moaned. He'd saved her life, maybe, that night he'd found her in the doorway. She had owed it to him to stick by him. I'm guessing he might be the father of Sarah's maybe-baby, as she calls it, abandoned even before the kid becomes real.

By the time she leaves, I am beginning to believe that she's probably lucky she got away from whatever is happening in that secret camp in the woods. Maybe "those people" aren't just a bunch of runaway kids living off the land. If they are something else, something evil or nuts, Sarah herself could be under the leaves right now. For some reason, she was afraid enough to run away from a place she thought was safe, to choose the streets again, to risk bothering a crabby old lady for a bowl of mac and cheese.

I am midway to sitting down in the overstuffed chair when I stop. I see in this same chair a girl in a red silk robe crying about a doll. I shake off the scene. *Not my business,* I answer myself, as usual, lowering my body into the cushion.

"No," I say out loud. "Not this time."

I should have asked more questions.

I push myself upright and hurry to the door. I look down the hall, hear my recycled red sneakers thumping down the stairs below me, the elevator occupied elsewhere. "Sarah!" I call, not caring that doors will open as my voice echoes down the stairwell. "Wait!"

CHAPTER TWELVE

JEFF

1997-1998

His clients say they like the way he talks, as if he's had an education. Jeff appreciates the way their money feeds his closet, his fridge, his stash. And he is okay with the whips and rings and giant plastic phalluses some of them require. He stores such equipment under his bed, next to the box of porn. Once Danny understands, after a long night of beer-inspired intimacy, the role Grandpa Jack had in Jeff's choice of profession, he and Danny don't talk about this other life or the men who walk through the dim lobby to his studio apartment and back into the street, past Danny, waiting on the steps outside.

Danny's at his door because his mother, pissed about the calls from school, has taken to laying into him the moment he walks in. He escapes her bourbon-fueled sermons by going to Jeff's. After the time he walked into a bare butt, not Jeff's, Danny waits until the john has climbed into his car or has walked briskly away. The apartment offers, besides a haven from his mother's voice, an assortment of goodies, which for Danny means pills of various colors.

"She kicked me out." This time Danny has come in carrying an old black suitcase. He sets it down and starts poking through the plastic bags Jeff keeps in a coffee can.

"Your mother says a lot of things, doesn't she?" Jeff lies on his bed, inhaling, letting the smoke ease out, a thin gray plume rising above his head. He pats the fifty bucks lying on the bed, still warm from the man's hand. "She won't."

"She found the bag of crack in my pocket."

"You still had it? God. Steve was waiting for it; he's already paid." Jeff sighs. He can't believe Danny has fucked up again.

Danny had stayed home that day—the flu, he told his mother. She shook her head and poured herself another drink. "Sure," was all she said. Then she picked up his jacket, felt the baggie in the pocket, took it out. When she screamed at him to get out, he did.

"Wasn't my fault. I just smoked a little, to test it. I was going to deliver the rest tomorrow before school. I still got the bag, so no loss." Danny nudges the suitcase at his feet. "I don't have any place to go."

"I thought we agreed." Jeff pushes himself up on one elbow. "We're in this to make money. Crackheads don't make money." That had been their first rule. They would sell, not use. Crack, especially. Pot and pills were cheaper, easier to come by, less profitable.

Jeff lies back down again, mellowing out, doesn't bother to look at Danny as he takes another drag and offers the reefer to his friend. "Your mother won't remember any of this in a couple of days. Let her cool off so you can plead adolescence. And stick with the plan: I find it, you deliver it.

The guy is so terrified he pees his pants, and he hands over his wallet with his eyes closed. Danny takes it, counts out eight $10 bills, tosses the rest on the ground. Jeff is disappointed. Eighty bucks is hardly worth the effort. "Let's check his pockets." He opens his jacket and pulls the knife out of its sheath, aims it at the man's heart. "There's got to be more," he says.

"No more." The man, his forehead shiny with sweat, turns out his pants pockets, pats his tweed jacket, his hands shaking, forcing themselves into the narrow openings. "Nothing."

Danny bends to check for bills hidden in socks, but stops patting. "Wet. Forget it," he says. "It's enough for now."

One more jab at the white shirt reveals a little skin. The blade rests under the folds of his chin. "No sounds for ten minutes, or we're back to finish you for good." The man, his face ghostly pale in the dark of the doorway, nods, clutches his arms across body, lean against the window at his back. "Okay," he gasps.

Jeff and Danny run down the quiet street, abandoned now that the theater crowd has cleared, giving each other congratulatory shoves, laughing. *God, this is so easy,* Jeff thinks, *a new kind of thrill even if it is only eighty bucks. The look on the guy's face!* A few blocks away they turn a corner, stop, breathing hard. Grinning, Jeff slips the knife back into its holder at his waist. "Good piece of steel, this," he says. "Where'd you get it?"

Danny shrugs. "Kitchen drawer. Been there forever."

"Your mom will never miss it." They punch each other again. It is true; Danny's mother never misses anything.

"Let's go back to my place. We both deserve a night off."

This client reminds him of Grandpa Jack, a little older, "portly," his grandfather would have said. And rich. This afternoon is the third time he's come by, their next appointment set as he buttons his jacket, stretches his leathery neck to adjust his tie. Each time he's paid with $50 bills, one more with each visit.

Jeff spreads the three bills like a spray of winning cards and wonders how long this can go on. He enjoys talking to the old guy, would have listened even longer, but Roger says he has to get home.

"Wife, you know," as indeed Jeff does know. Roger's stories invariably involve his family life, kids in college, disappointment in bed. "That's why I'm so glad to have met you. You're good for me." He touches Jeff's arm, seems about to come closer, but does not. Jeff is relieved. The one thing he doesn't do is kiss. Never did like kisses, although he doesn't know for sure because no one has ever kissed him. Not that he can remember.

"You're good for me, too, Roger. See you next week." Roger opens the door and has to step around

Danny. He turns his face away and hurries down the stairs without looking back.

"What are you doing here? It's really late." Jeff starts to close the door. He needs a little quiet after a long day, not late-night pot-induced camaraderie.

"I need to come in. Something's happened." Danny tosses a newspaper at Jeff, goes to the closet and pulls out the coffee can containing the marijuana. "I almost killed my mother."

"Local Man Dies After Assault and Robbery, " Jeff reads aloud. He scans the article at the bottom of the front page which tells of a robbery victim who made his way into a store after being attacked and managed to describe his assailants and even their weapon, an ivory-handled hunting knife, before he died of a heart attack on the floor of the 7-Eleven as the medics arrived.

"Fuck."

"Mom knew it was us. She called the cops this time. She was going to report us before we actually murdered someone, she said. Teach us a lesson."

"The cunt."

"I hit her." Danny's words were coming out in lumps, between gulps for air.

Jeff has trouble making sense of what his friend is trying to say, but he knows it isn't good. "Take a breath," he says, dreading what might come next.

"I was so mad, I kicked her while she was screaming on the floor, and I was packing to get out of there when the cop knocked on the door."

By now, Danny is crying and mumbling something about the policeman asking about a "family disturbance." Something about her saying she'd been so upset she called the police. But by mistake, she told the cop. They'd made up. "We don't need you anymore. I'll take care of my son," she said. The cop asked if she was sure. "Yes," she answered, one hand bloody, pressing her nose. "I was careless, that's all."

Danny drags on a joint, and his words stutter to a stop. He takes another hit, rubs the frown between his eyes. "Why would my mother do that, lie like that?"

Jeff shakes his head. How could he know? "Your mom was drunk when she made the call, and by the time the cop came, she was still drunk and bloody and worried he'd think whatever had gone down was her fault. Maybe she was feeling guilty."

"I told her I hated her and I'd get even with her for everything. When I left, she was still moaning, holding her ribs." Danny is threatening to break up again, and Jeff has trouble understanding why. The woman has been a bitch of a mother. What's there to cry about when a parent sucks so bad at the job?

Later, after Danny had retreated into a sodden sleep on the couch, Jeff tried to figure it out. He certainly hadn't shed a tear when, a few months after he moved out, he got word that Grandpa Jack had hung himself. He was asked to come to his grandfather's room in a transient hotel to clear it out.

The smell had been nauseating because it had taken several days for his grandfather to be missed. Jeff almost turned back, but curiosity sent him into the room, his jacket collar over his nose. He found no note, just a pile of books marked "My Grandson," which Jeff gave to the woman who came to clean the room.

He was leaving when she held out a folded piece of paper. "Want this?" she asked. "Fell out of one of the books." Jeff opened it, read the words, shoved the letter in his pocket. Grandpa Jack had saved it. Why? He'd think about it later. Right then, he needed to close the door on what was left of his grandfather.

Lonely or guilt-stricken? Didn't matter to anyone but a useless old man. Certainly not, he thinks, to the old man's grandson, who still sometimes waits for the mattress to move, the blankets to lift and bring in cold air and warm hands. *Fuck him.*

Jeff wakes Danny up. Then he opens the closet where his clothes and his backpack wait. "Doesn't mean that she won't sober up and call the police again, does it? We're out of here." The OxyContin he swallowed a few minutes before is kicking in, and he grins at Danny, who is blowing his nose on toilet paper, done with the tears. "I'll miss Roger, but there will be a lot more Rogers up north in Green River. And good business for you, too. You'll see."

CHAPTER THIRTEEN

MATT

SEPTEMBER 2009

The street is a familiar one. A woman has reported a body in a gutter, covered with leaves. He drives slowly, until he sees the flashing lights of the EMT half a block away.

As a patrolman, Matt Trommald had been assigned to this neighborhood. By day, the small park accommodated then, and still does, drug dealers, transients slumped on the wooden benches along the paths, mothers with strollers, and teenagers looking for a place to land. At 11:00 P.M. it officially closes. The benches are empty. However, the patches of grass and bark dust away from the lights, hidden in shadows, echo with the sounds of kids sharing their alcohol, drugs, sex, and laughter. Most live in the apartments that line the streets, Matt guessed. The park provides an escape from family and walls. With his flashlight and loudspeaker, some nights Matt would send a dozen or more kids streaming into the dark yelling obscenities and threats as they ran. Different kids, now, but the same vocabulary, he is sure.

He pulls up, lights on, in the middle of the street. A couple of kneeling medics stand up, and he sees a body lying in the debris in the gutter. He gets out, walks to the crowded curb.

"Dead, , looks like for couple of days," a medic says.

Dry oak leaves flutter and rise in a light breeze, and an arm is revealed. A shoulder, an ear pressed against a bloody head. He can see that the victim was young, twenty, maybe, with not only a head wound but a cut that has left a red trail across the front of his plaid flannel shirt. The medical examiner will follow in a minute or two with a photographer. When they're finished, he'll search pockets, attempt to learn who this kid is. Was.

When the body is ready to be taken to the morgue, Matt stoops to look through pockets, turns him slightly to inspect arms, the other half of his face. One tattoo, done with a needle and a ballpoint pen, a smiley face, is embedded in the skin on the back of his left hand. Jeans, a knee patched with a plaid material similar to the shirt he is wearing. Brown hair, shoulder length, held back in a rubber-banded pony. Fingernails grimy, hands dirty. Athletic shoes, worn but tied. No wallet, one pocket turned out as if someone had pulled something out of it. A good-looking kid. No sign of gang identity, more likely a street kid, killed for whatever was in that pocket.

Matt stands up and realizes he has company, mostly older folks. Neighbors. "Anyone know this person?" Heads shake. Matt hands out his card. "If you hear anything, give me a call. We'll need your help." The cards are glanced at, held between fingers like unwanted gifts as the small crowd moves on.

"It's that damn park." A balding, elderly man grabs Matt's arm. "They ought to bulldoze it, get rid of the shit that goes on there. How's a person supposed to sleep knowing they're killing people a block away?" Murmurs. Matt wants to reassure him but doesn't. The man isn't really asking a question, only making a comment about life.

One of those people walking away might have been the person who made the 911 call. An older voice, female, refused to identify herself. Matt pauses. Why would an innocent bystander not give her name? What did she see that would make her either afraid or not so innocent? Hard to think that any one of the slow-stepping seventy-year-olds had either the strength or the reason to murder the boy who is now being lifted onto the gurney.

He radios his desk, asks his assistant, Shelly, if she has been able to trace the call. She has. It came from the multistory low-income apartment house Matt can see a block away. He gets out his pad, jots down the phone number and waits for the name of the person he'll be talking to in a minute or two.

"Only problem is," Shelly continues, "it's a public phone, used by any number of renters. The bill goes to the Housing Authority."

Inside the building, the same old guy who wanted to bulldoze the park is yelling into the phone as Matt approaches. "Yeah, a murder. Probably drug wars. It's hell here, Bobby." He listens for a moment, eyes downcast, and Matt hears him add softly, "Are you sure? I wouldn't be any trouble." Then, "Okay, then." The hand that hangs the phone back in its cradle trembles. The other hand clutches a spray can of disinfectant and a washcloth. He sprays and wipes the phone, turns and sees Matt.

"I do this every time, before and after. Just to make sure. You never know who's been using this thing." He rubs the cloth over his hands and shuffles toward the elevator.

No fingerprints. No way of finding out that way who the woman is. "Just a minute," Matt calls. The elevator doors ding and open, and he and the man step in. "Were you near the phone or in that hall an hour ago? We need to know who used the phone about that time."

"Police, huh? No, but as long as I got you here, explain to me why the park is allowed to . . ."

The doors open and Matt escapes. The doors close behind him, and he spends a few moments exploring the hall. Judging by the numbers on the doors, there are maybe thirty residents on each of ten floors. Impossible. Maybe forensics will be able to identify the kid, get word back to whoever is still thinking about him, worrying about him.

Matt heads back to the station, signs out, says, "Great" when Shelly asks how Collin is doing. Matt hesitates at the door, pleased that she has bothered to ask.

Collin graduates this week from the Academy. He'll always be a little different, but his difference has become okay—in fact, better than okay. He's almost a genius at computers. He makes Matt laugh. He has taught Matt what love is. Matt smiles at the thought. Then a boy's face, almost buried in oak leaves, a kid just about the same age as Collin, comes into focus. That unknown boy most likely taught a parent what love was also. And now he'll teach that parent what sorrow is.

CHAPTER FOURTEEN

JEFF

APRIL 2000

Yes, there are other Rogers up north in Green River, quite a few, Jeff is relieved to discover after the first uneasy weeks of learning the ropes in the large city lounging on the bank of a lazy, tourist-blooming river.

Finding a place to sleep wasn't difficult if Jeff and Danny wanted to spend their nights in the bushes of a park or on a bench near the city center. They were safe from the cops who were looking for two almost-murderers. No one could find them in the muddle of transients wandering the paths, lying on the grass, sleeping under rough wool blankets in the midst of the parade of friendly or frightened or astonished mid-western visitors, their arms full of souvenirs from the boutique shops that line the streets.

Then they got beds in a shelter and food in a youth agency that offered them showers and advice to get their GEDs. That lasted until they decided, high on crystal meth, that they disliked the attitude of a snoring bunkmate and pulled him out of bed and would have maybe killed him had the night counselor not heard his yells. On the street the next morning, they knew two things: meth makes them mean, and they need money.

Jeff finds a clean pair of pants in his pack, lifts the collar, Brando style, of his leather jacket, and is turning a trick in a gray Volvo fifteen minutes later. Danny learns that meth is the drug of choice in the parks, buys an ounce, sells it in eight balls for twice as much as he paid, to businessmen in suits on the sidewalk in front of the Y and scabby teenagers on benches in several parks and lots of folks in between. The partners begin to bring in enough money to pay the rent on a furnished room over a storefront. The bed isn't bad, and they eat fast food and support their need for pot-enhanced munchies with Cheetos and chips. Life seems okay.

Their room becomes a gathering place for kids they meet on the streets, and some nights four or five teenagers sink back into the old sofa and chairs, smoke, laugh, drink 40s, and tell stories. These evenings have rules. Jeff, aware of the need to protect his and Danny's new life, enforces them. Noise down, arguments civil, fighters will be thrown out. "Bring your own stuff, but no meth, no tweaking, no out-of-control behavior. This is a safe place," he says. He likes that word. Reminds him of his first meeting with Grandpa Jack, how good *safe* felt, at first.

So, nightly, kids stoked on pot brag about how they ended up on the street, how they manage to survive, and sometimes, how they will escape. Everyone has a story and everyone has a dream, and those dreams intrigue Jeff. He has a few dreams of his own, always has had. Dreams separate us from the animals, Grandpa Jack used to lecture, and Jeff likes that idea. He asks questions, encourages these ragtag visionaries. Danny just listens, mostly.

"I been hustling two years now," a thin, almost-handsome red-haired boy, Squirrel, tells them. "Escorting, I call it. I need money, like everybody, and it comes easy now."

"Bareback?" Jeff asks.

"For enough extra."

"A little dangerous, isn't it?"

Squirrel shrugs. "Maybe. Who knows?" Squirrel closes his eyes and sucks on a roach someone hands him. "I don't worry much anymore," he adds, his voice thin, not quite convincing, holding smoke and worry inside. Jeff nods. He's been there.

A girl's voice interrupts. "I been prostituting a year and I'm thinking of getting out. An acquaintance of mine got Hep C shooting up, and she's still working." Her brown breasts wobble between her shoulders and her waist. She presses them against her knee as she slips off her shoe, a metallic gold stiletto. "I don't think that's right, do you? Being sick and giving it to other people?" She sits back up and looks at Jeff.

He points to the tracks on her arm. "How about you? Are you sick?"

"Just the usual. I get looked at every month or so at the clinic. My pimp insists on it. This is like a job to me. I'm careful." As if her story might not be believable, she goes on: "You know, I don't get off with a john. While he's busy, my mind is somewhere else, and my eyes are on his wallet." She bends her arm, hides the scars. "And I don't shoot up anymore, either. Like I said, I'm looking for a way out of here." She leans forward again to pat the German shepherd dozing at her feet and to recover her shoe. "But for now, I got to go to work," she says, rising up, adjusting her heavy boobs, sending a grin to the circle of faces around her.

Jeff likes this girl, Kitten. She is tough enough to live her dream, with a little luck. But not with her best friend, the dog that has kept her from being able to escape into one of the shelters in town. No animal is worth that; Jeff would off him in a minute if it meant getting a regular bed and a shower. Kevin the Dog stirs as if he knows what Jeff is thinking, then lumbers up and follows his mistress as she teeters toward the door.

The two girls sitting next to each other on the floor release the hands they have been holding to let Kitten and Kevin get by. Then they share a bottle of beer, one chugging and then handing it to the other. Queers. The label bothers Jeff. He doesn't think of himself as queer, but maybe bi if he had to give himself a label. He does get off with most of his clients. But he also likes to think about women sometimes. Kitten, for instance. He isn't sure he'd hold a man's hand or anything else if money weren't involved. A drag on his pipe subdues a familiar rush of anger. Unless it is his grandfather, and he is ten years old again. Unless something more than money is involved.

"Kicked out," one of the girls explains. "There's lots of us out there."

"And some who claim they're lesbians so they don't get raped where they're squatting."

"That's not us." They connect hands again and lean into each other.

Danny has been quiet all evening, watching and listening as usual. "It's good to have some friends," he says, when everyone is gone and he and Jeff are picking up the bottles and cans and cleaning out the cereal bowls they used as ashtrays. They both are a little high, and Danny does not pull away when Jeff slips an arm over his shoulder.

"Don't worry," Jeff says. "I'll be your best friend no matter what."

He feels good when Danny grins, says, "Sure. Me too."

CHAPTER FIFTEEN

SARAH

SEPTEMBER 2009

I stop on the bottom step. "Wait," Ellie calls again. I turn around, run up the two flights, dragging my bag behind me, to where she stands, hands on hips. I don't expect a hug, although I'd like to give her one.

"If you're going to be staying a few days more, we have to go to the food bank," Ellie says as she lets me in the door, like nothing special's happened.

Besides the day-old bread and canned beans on the shelves, the bins bulge with bags of potatoes and ears of corn, their tassels brown and wilted. "They're still good," Ellie decides, after she's pulled back the husks on a couple of them. "Maybe we can find some butter in the cooler." We do, and we also find a thawed turkey that needs to be cooked fast.

"I love turkey," I say.

"That's good, because we'll be eating it for a week." Ellie unloads the cart and counts out the food stamps in her wallet. Then we get on the bus, glad to find a couple of empty seats. We don't talk much, just hang onto our bags when the bus leans around corners.

That night we have an early Thanksgiving feast and eat it sitting on the davenport, watching the news. During a commercial, she catches me eyeing the picture of the good-looking guy on the table, but I don't say anything.

"He's my son," she says.

"He has a nice smile." Maybe her smile if she'd ever smile. "How old is he?"

"Twenty-eight. I haven't seen him in a long time." She doesn't explain, and I can tell that's all I'm going to get. She's just the opposite of me, a mother abandoned by a child, not vice versa. Probably it feels the same.

"Starkey is twenty-eight," I say, trying to keep the conversation going.

"The camp guy?" She puts her fork down.

So I describe Starkey, how his chin is covered with a short, neat beard, how he wears a gold earring in one ear, and how he knots a bandanna around his head like a pirate. "Pirate eyes, too," I add, "like he can see what we're thinking."

"Yeah?" she says.

"Nine of us when I was up there. One of the girls, Lila, hangs with Mouse. She looks Chinese or something, tiny and pretty; he's black or maybe half black, quiet except when he's talking to her. They've been together for a while. Owl, the other girl, is slow and stays by herself mostly, except when one of the guys teases her. Then she yells and hits back." A trickle of sad makes me blink when I think of those kids, especially Leaky and Jimmy.

"Leaky's gay. You know that the minute you meet him. And Jimmy makes everyone laugh, but he's pretty brave, like the night Peter and him saved me. He gets teased because he's fat, like Leaky does because he's queer, and Peter stood up for both of them."

It feels kind of good to talk about Peter, how we shared a sleeping mat and how we whispered half the night about our lives. Sometimes I would massage his back, my fingers pushing into the rough scars that crisscrossed his shoulders as he talked about leaving home, about his adventures the year he was on his own. One night he told me about the attack in a camp under the bridge. The scars, he explained. He didn't tell me everything. He just said, "This place is better, especially with you here."

And I told him my story. I told him everything, and when I cried, he would touch me, too.

Ellie hands me a Kleenex. I blow my nose.

"Starkey?" she asks.

Now that I'm away from the camp, I have trouble believing that those fire-flicked scenes were real. But when I close my eyes, I can see and hear it all. I keep talking and remembering.

Starkey leans back into the canvas chair, looking at us through the smoke, smiling in a kindly way, his hand in his lap, fingers moving a little.

"How old were you, Leaky, when you realized you liked it in the ass?"

"I don't remember." Leaky's soft voice floats above the cinders in front of him.

"Really?" Starkey answers. "I remember that moment quite clearly. I bet you do, too." Then he turns to Lila. "Stepfather, right? What did he like?"

Lila looks down, mumbles a few words.

"Speak up, girl—I'm asking about your stepfather. Has nothing to do with you." Starkey raises his chin, turns his ear toward her.

"Sometimes he went in. Other times he wanted me to suck him."

"Swallow?"

Lila nods. "Yeah. He said it was good for me." Her face didn't move, except for her eyelids, which lowered then widened, sending her dark gaze into the trees.

I'm getting to the bad part of this story. I can't look at Ellie because her face has folded into misery. She holds her hand up to stop me. She says she needs to take a break, and she gets up to pour hot water over instant coffee. She brings me a cup. When she sits back down, she looks into her coffee and asks why anyone would share secrets with a pirate.

"Because he shared his secrets with us," I answer, relieved to be sent on a different track.

I remember his voice when he explained why he wanted to know about us, our experiences. He leaned forward in his chair, looking us over, capturing our eyes. "I know what you've gone through," he said. "My grandfather called me his poontang, a Southern expression. I thought it meant he loved me."

"We laughed because he was laughing."

"This Starkey is crazy," Ellie says. "Laughing about kids getting hurt, himself getting hurt." She puts down her cup with a *thump* on the end table.

I'm not finished. I'm still remembering.

"Some nights Starkey doesn't laugh," I say.

"'When I ask you to do something, I expect it to happen immediately.' Those nights he walks around our circle flapping a leather belt like a whip. It lands on someone who hasn't brought back enough food or on someone who's missed cleanup duty, once on me because I hadn't gathered enough wood to keep the fire going until morning."

"A belt! Don't tell me anymore." Ellie leans back against the quilt, eyes closed, but I can tell she's listening. And I keep on.

"Like I said before, Starkey asked us to prove our loyalty to the family. 'Courageous tasks,' he called them. At first they were easy, but then they got harder: stealing a six-pack of beer; robbing a panhandler of his change and his sign; painting mailboxes with penises, maybe; a silver knife slashing into something; a cuss word. Warnings that those blocks belonged to Starkey, just like the woods were his."

Ellie opens her eyes, looks at me. "The *Mom* heart. The one I couldn't understand?"

"That was Jimmy's mark. He misses his mom a lot. She's in prison, but she's not a bad person, like his father says every time her name comes up. And she loves him—that he knows for sure."

Ellie leans back again. The story oozes out of me, like dirty water from a rusty Dumpster. No way to stop it.

I tell her how Jimmy was the first to get hit with a fist. He had complained about the smell of the camp, said they should have some rules about where they could piss and all. Starkey swung at him and Jimmy went down. "Who is in charge here? Not you, you fat pansy. Anymore suggestions?"

Jimmy whispered "No" through the blood and the tooth he spit out.

"Good. Now go out and dig a latrine since you're the one who brought it up." He handed him a big spoon and Jimmy went off to find a good place.

Then I tell how Lila got it next. She'd been holding out on the stuff she swiped in the convenience stores. Starkey found the wrappers from fruit bars in her sleeping bag. This time he insisted that her boyfriend, Mouse, discipline her, and she just stood there and let him slap her. "Again," Starkey yelled. And Mouse did.

Then Peter got up, stood in front of Starkey at the fire. "This isn't right. Families should take care of each other."

"What a concept! Like this?" Starkey shoved him, and Peter fell into the flames. Sparks flew all over us. Laughing his big pirate laugh, Starkey pulled

Peter out, brushed him off, and said, "This is how I learned to take care of my family." Then we heard a little more of Starkey's past, the beatings his father gave him for breathing, the broken arm, the bruises his teachers would ask about.

"I never told anyone," he said, "because I knew that my father wanted me to grow up tough and ready to take whatever happened no matter what, even when it meant letting my grandfather treat me like a whore. My father had endured it and so would I, he told me the one time he called me from prison. And I did. I learned to respect my old man and still do, wherever he is. He was strong. That's why I'm tough on you guys. Life's going to treat you bad. Already has. And I'm toughening you up."

Then Starkey rubbed Mouse's head and nodded at Lila. "We're in combat training here. By the time I've finished with you, you'll be ready to take on whatever you get handed."

"Shit," Ellie says.

My throat hurts from imitating Starkey's voice. I take a sip of coffee. I have only a little more to tell, but it's the worst part. This memory is too real to just be a memory. I arrange my words so that she can see it like I can. I smell the campfire and my stomach squeezes, just like that night.

"Peter is sitting next to me, his fingers touching mine. Leaky and Jimmy huddle together on the sleeping bag. The other kids look at their feet, glad maybe that Starkey is smiling, his hands open, empty.

"Starkey says that the time has come to truly test our loyalty to the family. The next task will tell the tale. 'Two of you,' and he's looking at me and Peter, 'will go down to the town and come back with proof that you have gotten rid of one demented street person. Worthless detritus,' he says, 'of no value to anyone. This will be a true test of your intestinal fortitude. You will bring back a trophy. A finger.'

"I don't breathe under his pirate stare. 'Two nights from now, we'll draw straws to determine who will be chosen for this great honor.'"

"A finger," I repeat. "That's when I know I have to leave. I don't tell Peter I am going. I don't want him in trouble when Starkey finds out I am gone. I just left."

I start crying, and I take Ellie's hand in mine, whether she likes it or not.

CHAPTER SIXTEEN

MATT

2003-2006

The woman turns, kisses Matt lightly on the cheek. A twitch of her lips means *I'm sorry,* but she says, "Thanks for having me over. We should do it again sometime." She turns away, steps down the stairs of his porch as her last words float up to him. He won't see her again, he knows. An evening with his son is usually enough to convince most women they should move on.

Matt closes the door, glances at the twelve-year-old whose thumbs are moving at the speed of sound over the box in his hand. The boy does not look up. He probably does not know that his father's friend has left. Nor does it seem he cares. Only *Modern Warfare 2* matters. Three stars, best he's ever done, he says when he finally raises his eyes.

"Time for bed."

Collin doesn't respond.

"You have a choice. Bed in ten minutes or no games tomorrow. It's up to you."

The boy's thumbs slow, then pick up speed. "Ten," he says, not looking up.

Matt breathes, goes to the kitchen to clean up the kitchen. No fight tonight, maybe. He's never sure, but he's learning to manage the mercurial nature of his son, to avoid the confrontations that sometimes still lead to meltdowns, to enjoy the accomplishments of this child who struggles daily to find himself. In electronic games, mostly. Collin is very good at them. His focus is phenomenal, his delight contagious.

As Matt closes the dishwasher door, he hears the toilet flush. Collin is getting ready for bed. In the morning he'll go to school, stay there until he is picked up. Grandma Grace, living in her own apartment again, is backup now that life is calmer. She is getting pretty good at Nintendo. And she knows how to get her grandson to bed on those nights Matt works late, usually with cookies and a story. Grace has a lover, a nice old guy who smiles a lot as he walks hand-in-hand with her. She smiles a lot, too, and Matt is envious. He's certain he'll not be walking close to someone for a long time. Not after tonight, another replay of a scene he's had a part in more than once, Collin the main character.

A hand touches him. "Goodnight, Papa," his son says. Then the boy swirls away, before Matt can hug him. Collin still doesn't like hugs much.

Over the next three years, they work out a system, he and Grace. An email a day outlines each of their schedules. Texting allows for deviations. Grace moves in with Ben, Grandpa Ben to Collin. The disparate parents fill in the spaces in Collin's day like cotton balls, benign but supportive. Collin spends most of his time in his sophomore special-ed classes and with Leslie, his therapist, who continues to work with him on his "people skills," as she calls them.

Matt has tried to help Collin practice these skills by encouraging him to invite someone from school to play his games. When one boy finally accepts Collin's invitation, Matt watches from the kitchen. The boys sit at the coffee table, their hands working the controls. The excited laughter and a "shit" or two is music to Matt's ears, until he interrupts their concentration with Cokes and he sees that his son is talking too much and not listening, and watches the other boy yawn and roll his eyes, turn away, finger the box in his lap, waiting to get back to the action and away from Collin.

Each time Collin manages to get someone to come over, probably bribed by his collection of games, the would-be friend invariably walks away, seemingly relieved.

Matt stops trying to influence his son's social life. Collin, he finally understands, doesn't do intimacy, either in words or in the exchange of nonverbal communication that is the habit of teenagers. Sometimes, though, the boy doesn't cringe when Matt hugs him. And lately, Collin, besides displaying a gift for electronic devices, is showing an impatience with parental direction. A typical fifteen-year-old, almost.

"Hey, Collin!" Matt opens the front door, his stomach growling with the aroma of the pepperoni pizza he's carrying. Usually when he comes home, his son is sitting in the lounger in the living room involved in a game, a soda by his side. This evening Collin hasn't texted Grace to say he's arrived home, but sometimes he forgets. But he's not in his room either. The house is quiet, empty.

Matt calls Grace. She hasn't heard from her grandson. Perhaps he's gone to the store for something. Or to a friend's house; she's forgotten that

Collin doesn't have friends he would visit, but perhaps his teacher would know? Matt calls the school, gets a register of numbers, calls Collin's teacher, Barbara Edgerton. Collin had been in school, through his last class, had walked out as usual, his teacher checking to make sure he had his backpack, and assignments. She hadn't noticed anything unusual as he walked through the school's doors toward the bus waiting for him at the curb, as it always did.

Matt forces himself not to panic. A kid could go out for a while to get a DVD, to pick up a pizza to back up what his father will come up with for dinner. He waits fifteen minutes, then goes out the door and wanders the stores in the neighborhood. When he comes back, the apartment is as empty as it was when he left it. He dials the school, gets the bus company's phone number.

"My son hasn't come home," he says, hoping not to sound too anxious. "I need to know if he got on the bus at the school. And if he got off it at the usual corner." He's put on hold for five minutes before he's told that as far as the driver remembers, Collin did not get on the bus. In fact, the driver waited a minute or two before he gave in to the demands from the back of the bus to get moving, it was hot.

He figured maybe Collin's parents or somebody had picked him up.

Grace and Matt drive to the school, fan out over the blocks around it. Ben will stay at home by the phone. They can't imagine he's gone far. He's still leery about using public transportation although his therapist has worked with him using the ticket machines, reading the maps, and has gone on a trip or two with him. Matt looks through the window of the 7-Eleven where Collin has shopped by himself. It is empty of customers. He asks. The counterman has not seen him. He goes by the other closed shops in the small mall and walks behind the building where the Dumpsters are kept. Except for a slinking cat, nothing moves. He walks to the edge of the park three blocks from the school.

This two-acre green space is well lit, a requirement when the city proposed it. The neighborhood also had input on the design. "We need a dog run and we need good lighting at night to keep the druggies out. Swings and climbing structures, of course, but no water feature. Attracts too many kids from outside our neighborhood; we don't need a circus around here."

Matt follows a winding path edged by benches and tall lights with a terrible sense of dread. He's done this sort of walk once before. Not looking for his son, of course, but looking for someone else's son, a raving kid with a gun in his hands. Thirteen years ago, another father looked for a damaged kid, fear padding his steps.

Voices off to the side make him stop, listen. A girl, a boy. And a blanket, he sees as he makes his way past a rhododendron. Two pairs of annoyed eyes glare at him from the shadows. "Sorry," he says. He wishes it were his son with his hand on the girl's breast.

He can hear traffic at the far edge of the park. Car lights flash through the shrubs and trees. Empty benches line up along the path. He stops because he's not sure where to go next. When his cell phone rings, he knows Grace has found Collin. Except she hasn't.

"Now what?" she asks.

He tells her to go home. He'll do the same, and he'll report Collin missing even though it has been only a few hours. Perhaps his rank will get a search started before the required twenty-four hours have passed. His team will understand. They are very aware of the silent boy who has visited the precinct with his father over the past ten years. Each of the officers, all family people, has an inkling of what the detective's life must be like.

Matt sits for a minute on the last bench before the entrance to the path. Five breaths. Through his nose. Sometimes it still works.

A rustling in the leaves means an animal is moving somewhere behind him. A cat, probably, or a rabbit. People drop rabbits in this park all the time, pet rabbits left to mow down the grass and make baby rabbits. It was in the paper recently. He turns.

No rabbit under that bush. A huddle of a body, moving ever so slowly, its breaths silent sobs, a familiar tapping of fingers, a son.

"Collin."

This time Collin lets his father hold him.

When he's calmer, he says he wants to go home.

It is Grace who gets the story out of her grandson, once the soda and pizza have done their job and Collin is sitting on the sofa, his fingers busy as usual. She sits next to him, asks, "What?"

"I can't stand it," he says in his halting way. "They call me names. They are mean. They bump into me in the hall. They laugh when I get mad and hit back. Today they grabbed my backpack, threw it in the garbage. I feel like a nothing." He doesn't cry, but his voice grates with despair. "I want to be invisible." He sinks lower into the cushions, and he doesn't look at Grace or his father. "You don't understand," he says.

Grace does not touch him but leans toward his closed eyes. "We hear you, Collin. We will fix this." Grace looks at Matt, gives him her mother-look. *Tonight*, it says. *We will fix this.*

Matt is still working on breathing. What if Collin had lain in the bushes until morning, had gotten up confused, had gone into one of his now seldom meltdowns, had raged and screamed at whoever found him, had had a person with a gun come toward him . . . What if? His chest rises, falls. He can't stand what he is imagining.

As if she could read his thoughts, Grace takes his hand, squeezes his fingers, and says, "Matt, it's over. We're going to be okay."

Damn, he thinks. *My mother.*

Grace and Matt get Collin to bed. The boy will not return to the local high school in the morning. They will find a place that fits his needs, a school where he can be himself, whatever that is.

CHAPTER SEVENTEEN

JEFF

2002

And Danny and Jeff *are* the best of friends for the next year or so. Both the escorting business and the drug business are successful enough for them to rent a place with a small kitchen and room enough for Jeff to bring regular clients over, once he's bought new sheets and they've painted the living room. The apartment looks out over a quiet street, and on a clear day they can see a snow-touched mountain range against the sky, hear the sounds of the city shimmering in the foreground.

At first Danny goes down to the park to re-up his drug supply, and he spends time at a couple of well-known corners selling it, but once he gets a cell phone, he is freed up to have customers all over the riverfront area and in some of the neighborhoods. The only hitch in the arrangement is the nights Jeff needs the apartment and Danny has to find some-where else to spend time. Jeff shrugs, impatient with his roommate when he complains about having to sit at a bar three blocks away, drinking cheap well drinks and waiting for Jeff's phone call to let him know that the way is clear to come home. "Without a little inconvenience once in a while, we'd be sleep-ing under a bush. Fred and the others pay very well, as you know."

And Jeff is dressing well, designer jeans, silk shirts, and a clinging Mario leather jacket, a gift from a cli-ent, as he has taken to calling his johns. His precise haircut requires weekly stops at the Bob Bar. The look attracts the sort of men who drive through the neighborhood in luxury sedans. Jeff invites these men into his apartment, once he knows they want to go steady, that is, see him on a regular schedule. The parking lot in back of the building is behind a fence, discreet, usually safe from teenager prowlers if the cars are empty of tempting cargo.

It seems only right that the bedroom is Jeff's because it is his business office. Danny's bed is the sofa in the living room, and he folds his blankets each morning and stores them in the closet. Jeff does most of whatever cooking they do, usually pizza or tacos and always a salad. Danny takes the laundry to the basement machines. Other chores—cleaning the toilet, sweeping the floors—are divided up without talking much about them. However, Danny's habit of leaving his newspapers scattered all over the living room and his inability to put his dishes into the washer really annoys Jeff. After a scene that involves the smell of sour milk and a labyrinth of magazines and paper as he and a client open the apartment door, Jeff blows.

"It's embarrassing leading someone into a rat's nest." Jeff isn't yelling, but he notices his next words make Danny's eyes widen. "You're a slob. Start picking up before you leave."

Danny glances at the table still piled with the morning paper, encrusted cereal bowls, and a couple of beer bottles from the night before. "Some of this mess is yours, Jeff. Or have I been promoted to cleaning lady also?" When Jeff ignores the question, he adds, "As far as your business goes, cooling my heels waiting for you to fuck some pervert is beyond the call of duty for a roommate. I'm sick of closing the Iron Horse every other night."

Jeff doesn't like the anger shaking Danny's voice, and he understands he has to do some compromising to keep things on track. Over a pizza and a couple of IPAs, they agree that Danny will clean up before he leaves in the mornings, and Jeff will schedule his appointments earlier. After all, they both want to live the good life they have begun. They have a trip to Mexico planned, a car picked out. All they need is a little more time, a few more steady customers. Their separate ways of making money don't conflict, really. Jeff doesn't do drugs much anymore, and Danny definitely doesn't do men. For a few months, things seem to be working out.

At Christmas time, on a whim, they buy a tree and decorations. Danny brings home a couple of bottles and some dope and invites a few people he knows to a spur-of-the-moment party. Jeff, who has good memories of the groups that used to gather in their apartment in McLaughlin, tells several guys he's met to come, too. It seems like a good idea until Jeff notices that the druggies are circling around the hustlers. He can see that goodwill to all good men isn't going to happen soon, no matter what anyone is swallowing or smoking.

Jeff squirms as voices get loud, and malevolent looks (a useful Grandpa Jack word at the moment) fly across the room, and when a mascaraed young man in spandex tights slaps a black kid whose eyes radiate disdain from under a hoodie, all hell breaks loose. Jeff ducks a couple of flying chairs as a mirror goes down along with several bodies before Danny and he are able to shove everyone out.

"Shit. What happened?" Danny asks, panting as he shuts the door and kicks at the debris at his feet. He fumbles a doobie out of his shirt pocket and manages to get it lit.

Jeff stops dumping pieces of mirror and chairs into a large plastic garbage bag, stands up. "This isn't working." This time he means it.

"What?"

"This." He points at the destroyed living room and then at Danny. "Fuck our big plans." Giving up those plans doesn't mean he can't have plans of his own, does it? To be free, to make his way alone, no Danny to complain, to hold him back. Exhilaration propels his words. "I want my own place. I don't need zoned-out jerks disrupting my life." He pushes an accusing finger against his roommate's shoulder, and Danny falls against the sofa to steady himself. "Including you. You've become a detriment. Not just tonight. Every night this week."

This feels so right, this letting loose of angry thoughts that have been festering for weeks. "I don't like living with a concoction of chemicals for a room-mate." Although he is a little drunk, he knows that what he is saying is the truth. "You are an addicted loser, my friend."

Danny straightens. His eyes are steady, almost sober, as he stares at Jeff. "Okay." A tight grimace captures his lips. Then he speaks, slowly, a rhythmic cadence, as if he's reading from a familiar script. "For your information, I'm having trouble living with a poontang, a guy who gets paid to be fucked by fat old men. No problem. And good riddance, asshole."

When he lurches by to get to his closet, his elbow catches Jeff on the nose. Jeff reacts to the pain without thinking, sends a fist into a soft crotch. They roll around on the floor until Danny lays a broken chair leg across Jeff's forehead. Jeff feels himself twitch in the midst of shards of mirror as he watches Danny pack his backpack, his drugs, and the few books he has collected.

Their friendship is as shattered as the mirror he's lying on, an apt metaphor, his grandfather would have said. Jeff moves his head and hears the glass crunch behind his neck. He needs to say something to acknowledge this moment. Something memorable. Nothing. As the door slams, he hears himself yell, "Your mom's a ho." Grandpa Jack's words are apparently lost in a swirl of pot and a cracked forehead and the emptiness of a room. He rolls over, raises himself up, and picks his way through the broken glass to the broom closet. He has time, while he sweeps, to wish he hadn't told Danny his grandfather's nickname for him.

The fat old man Danny referred to is Fred, a regular who has been in the apartment enough times to have crossed paths with Danny. But he is a *rich* fat old man, an important fact Danny didn't quite get. Of course, Danny's mother isn't a ho, at least as far as Jeff knows, but she is a sloppy drunk, and Danny is following her down that path. Like mother, like son.

The glass in a neat pile, he pauses to wipe his bloody nose on a paper towel, and he rejects his next thought, tossing it along with the crumpled paper. *Like grandfather, like grandson?*

No, he is into the life for the money only. When he has enough, he'll move on. This always was the plan, with Danny or without him. One of his customers told him he had a good voice, an actor's voice, and brought him a brochure about the Northwest Acting Academy. He can go to that school if he saves some money, works part-time, maybe finds another steady client who'll help. He has just finished cleaning up the living room, the garbage bag stashed behind the door in the closet, when his cell rings. It is Fred.

CHAPTER EIGHTEEN

ELLIE

SEPTEMBER 2009

Sarah's been on the davenport, hiding under a pillow, for two days, and she's driving me nuts. I have read the same page of *I is for Innocent* three times. "Go do the wash," I say. "Think about something else." I hand her the basket of clothes we've accumulated in the bathroom.

While she's gone, I have to plan. I close my book. Once and for all, she's got to go some place else. I'm sick to my stomach all the time. I can't go on listening to her terrible stories, the words that come out like a kitten mewling. I don't know what to say to someone who doesn't wear mascara anymore because it just runs off as soon as she puts it on. I don't know what to pat when I get the urge, and I end up sticking my hands between my knees. I'm not helping her, and I understand once again that I'm not good at taking care of anyone but myself, and sometimes I doubt that. Like right now.

I boil water for coffee and when I try to spoon out a teaspoon of instant, nothing comes up. *Shit. We're out of Folgers.* And money. My Social Security check won't come for three days and at this moment my last quarters are being shoved into the coin box of a dryer, half of which is filled with clothes not my own. The spoon scraping for grains of dried coffee makes my next move obvious.

Tomorrow we'll go to the Williams House down the street where the medical bus parks. They've got people who will know where Sarah can go for help. I wash out the coffee jar with the hot water, pour the yellow dregs into my cup.

I'm sitting down when Sarah shoves the door open with the basket, our stuff separated and folded. "Sorry I took so long. I had to wait for the cops to finish downstairs."

A knock on the door cuts her off. I answer it and a tall man looks back at me, smiling only a little. I can tell he's a cop from the bulge under his jacket. *Damn, how did they know I was the one who called 911 the other night? Serves me right.*

"Sergeant Trommald. May I come in for a minute?" He steps in before I can answer. "I have a few questions. First, I need your name." I feel Sarah pull back, go to the kitchen, but this visit isn't about the Nike in the leaves.

"Ellie Miller," I say.

The cop goes on. "A man has been found dead, beaten to death, in the entry of the building. A medical clinic receipt in his pocket gives a name and his address and notes about the treatment of a young woman whose identity isn't known." He looks past my shoulder. "One of the neighbors downstairs tells me that the only young girl in this building is staying in this apartment."

I hear Sarah close the refrigerator behind me.

"So could I meet her?"

That's why I can't stand neighbors. None of their business.

"Sure," I say, and call to her.

"Someone's dead?" she asks, poking a piece of baloney into her mouth and chewing in a disinterested, teenage way. I can see she doesn't want to get involved either.

"He may be a resident of this building. Bearded older man. Did you know him?"

Sarah stops chewing and swallows, her glance flicking my way. "Yeah, if it's Rick. He helped me once."

The cop looks at me. "How about you, Mrs. Miller?"

"I know Rick enough to know he is a good guy, a little crazy once in a while, but I like him."

"A loner?"

"Except when his voices visit. Yeah, a loner." *Like most of us in this building*, I almost add.

Sarah has slunk onto the davenport, waiting for what will come next, and there is more, I'm sure, since the sergeant is taking out a pencil. I motion for him to sit down. Sarah scooches over to give him room next to her.

He squints at us over his notebook. "This is the second murder this month in this area. Both transients."

"So not too high on the list?" Peter's murder didn't even make the local paper after the first one-inch column that someone tacked on the bulletin board in the hall.

The sergeant frowns. "All murders are important. Right now, I need someone to identify him. He's not a pretty sight. The folks downstairs aren't sure. I'd like you two to come down and take a look before he's moved on to the morgue." He pauses to let us understand that this is not an invitation we can refuse. He stands up and we follow him out the door to the elevator.

And when we get off, we see him, curled up under the stairs next to his cart as if he'd gone to sleep just before he got to his door. A trail of blood has followed him from the front door. He's crawled in from the sidewalk, somehow, his hands and legs red, wet, his face an unrecognizable mash of flesh, his beard matted against his neck.

A silver earring dangles from the one ear I can see—the silver star earring Sarah gave him a few days ago.

For a minute I think that Sarah sees it, too, for she gasps. But she is looking at Rick's hand. A stub of a finger leaks onto the linoleum.

CHAPTER NINETEEN

JEFF

2003

It would have been a good plan, saving his money, school, if Fred hadn't gotten weird a few months later. The first time he came though the doorway shaking like a dipso, the man couldn't talk, only grunt. He slammed the door shut, went to the windows, turned up a slat in the blinds and tried to look out.

"Turn off the light!" he whispered and Jeff did, his own heart racing a little. After a few minutes, Fred found a chair in the dark, slumped into it, and said that it was okay to switch on a lamp—the problem was over.

Jeff poured a finger of brandy from Fred's bottle waiting on a shelf for him and placed it between shaking fingers. "What?" he asked.

"I was tailed by a big black guy on the bus. He nudged me when I was standing ready to get off, said something like, 'Watch out,' to me as the door opened. I looked back and saw that he had gotten off behind me, was behind me." Fred swallowed, coughed, held the glass in two hands.

"Why were you on the bus?" *Who rides the bus these days, anyway, especially someone in a cashmere overcoat? Just asking for it,* Jeff thought, until Fred took another sip and answered.

"My wife has placed a tracking device in my car. I heard it ticking this morning. They tick, you know, if you listen. She suspects."

At first, his client's fears had amused Jeff. After all, the man was paying part of the rent, and Jeff could put up with a little oddness. "They don't tick, Fred. Believe me, I know." And he had told Fred an almost believable story involving a friend who wanted the goods on his stepmother. Fred had calmed down, appreciated the concern Jeff showed him, in a few minutes.

This evening, a week later, after Fred got off the bus at the World Coffee Shop, a couple of blocks from Jeff's apartment, far enough away that anyone interested in his movements would have to follow him down a couple of narrow dark streets and would be observed easily by Fred, he says that another man, this one in a black raincoat, also got off and paused at the coffee shop. Minutes later Fred looked back and saw the man walking behind him. Fred is babbling, wet-browed and panicked.

"Why CIA?" Jeff asks. He's getting a little impatient with Fred's nonsense.

"My wife. Her brother is in the Secret Service. He denies it, but no one travels like he does in a normal job. She suspects something and told him." Fred is sure the guy is still out there, waiting, or maybe even in the hall outside, listening with one of those electronic devices even as they speak.

"Fred, the CIA isn't interested in wives' suspicions. Unless you are involved in some sort of espionage yourself." It occurs to Jeff that other than being an accountant who comes quick, he doesn't know much about Fred. Maybe the guy is some sort of double agent or spy or terrorist. He takes back that thought. Fred is fat, rich enough to keep a lover, a man who doesn't know or care shit about anything beyond his anxious penis. Jeff unzips his client's tweed trousers, calms him down, sends him home no longer tremoring.

However, by the third time this scene is played, Jeff has become somewhat paranoid himself. "Next time," he says, "I'll meet you at the bus stop, walk you to my apartment." He does, and they see only a stray cat and a woman with a baby stroller on the opposite sidewalk.

"That's a cover, don't you understand? Who'd suspect a woman with a baby?" Fred insists as they enter the apartment. "You don't care about me, do you? You have to go out and confront her, find out who's paying her to harass me." Fred stands with his arms crossed across his broad front, his small black eyes blazing.

Blazing with what? Jeff wonders. The eyes have a familiar cast. His grandfather's eyes the last time they argued. Out-of-control crazy eyes. It is time to end all this, just like he had to with Grandpa Jack.

"Get out," Jeff says as he reaches for the doorknob.

Fred's trembling cheeks pale. "What?"

"Get out. Don't come back. You've gone rotten on me."

Fred goes from pale to red. "You faggot. After everything I've given you—I've been paying your way for months. I thought you cared about me. Like I did you. You can't do this."

Jeff was about to say *yes I can* when Fred begins to weep, big chesty gasps that seem to burst from a pit of pure anguish.

"Jesus, Fred."

Fred throws himself against Jeff, and Jeff can feel the fat stomach quivering, wracked by its god-awful sounds.

Enough.

Jeff unwinds the arms from his neck. "Stop," he orders. He uses the one threat that can shut the man up. "The neighbors will hear."

Breathing more slowly, Fred grinds to a stop. He doesn't look back as he opens the door and stumbles down the hall.

The door is ajar. Jeff looks out, can't resist calling out, "Be careful, Fred. The CIA is watching." He hears the elevator door close. *Nice ride while it lasted*, he thinks. *Now what?*

"You murderer!" The middle-aged woman, her red hair a matted halo, her neck loafing into a fur collar, doubles her fists and lunges at him. Jeff steps sideways and lets her through the doorway.

"Who are you?" He has a sinking feeling he already knows.

"Mrs. Fred Berger. And you are his infective. And I am Fred's. He told me everything, crying, asking me to forgive him. But it's too late. You've killed us both. You will have two deaths on your record, dozens more probably." At this point, Mrs. Berger's flushed face crumbles, emits a wail of anguish. "How could you continue to sell your body when you knew it was toxic?" She reaches out to grab his arm, misses, and instead stumbles onto the sofa. "We're going to die because of you."

Jeff sits down next to her, rests an arm at the back of her neck, and covers her mouth with his palm to shut her up. He leans into her ear, tells her that he is not the infective, if there is such a word. "Until Fred, I tested clean. And during our months of assignations, I insisted we use condoms despite your husband's objections. Maybe because of them. Isn't it possible that along with all that fat, Fred is also carrying a load of guilt he'd like to spread around?"

He tightens his grip on her face when she tries to shake her head. He feels her gasps under his fingers. He keeps talking. "Only makes sense if you are a little nuts." A woman like this burgundy-haired harridan, screeching she is going to punish him somehow, could easily drive a person over the edge.

"I think you are both a little nuts," he whispers as her fists flail at him now in a lackluster, defeated way. Her eyes protrude, water, close. He waits for a minute and then removes his hand from her mouth and nose and feels her chest rise as air rushes in. Three breaths later she pushes herself upright and wails, "You're going to get it!" She aims a flaccid fist at his cheek and stumbles her way to the door. "You wait and see. It won't be long."

It would have been very easy to kill her. Jeff goes to the sink to wash the hand that is still wet with the woman's saliva. Poison, paid assassins, fire? Mrs. Berger, her puffy eyes overflowing with liquid hatred, seems capable of any of those plans. A missed opportunity, perhaps. Her disappearance would certainly simplify things. At the moment, though, even her spit can do him in. Jeff scrubs both hands with soap. AIDs or not, that woman can scare the shit out of a person.

He needs to leave this place. He has to get himself back on track, find another Fred, one who wouldn't be reluctant about a condom or go schizo over a wife. However, most old men are weird, he's found. Beginning with Grandpa Jack. So maybe he is through with old men.

Besides, without Danny's and Fred's contributions, he won't be able to pay the rent at the end of month.

CHAPTER TWENTY

MATT

2006

The school's plush grounds are as impressive as the historic brick building they surround. Bright green grass, kids sitting in the shadows of oak trees, music flowing from a flute, a fluttering drum offering a little backbone to the melody. A paradise, Matt tells himself, an expensive, safe paradise. McKinley Academy will cost more than most good colleges, but his son will get through his days here under the watchful eyes of people who respect differences, value individuality, promote self-esteem.

That's what both the brochure and Mrs. Glisan, the entrance counselor, assure him and Grace and a reluctant Collin, who recovers his good spirits when he sees the computer room and the ten boys bending into the screens in front of them. "We look for our students' strengths and build on them. Two of our seniors will be interning in animation studios this summer. Another will be working with a start-up company as a programmer."

"Yeah? Programming what?" Collin doesn't quite look at Mrs. Glisan, but his straight back signals his interest.

The woman sighs. "The way I understand it, a small company has developed an idea for helping companies keep track of individual state and county taxes so Internet sales companies will know instantly what to charge customers, tax-wise, and what they will owe the individual states and other governments in taxes."

The explanation seems to please Collin. He smiles for the first time this morning. Matt hasn't understood the woman, but the look on Collin's face tells him something more important. This will be Collin's school for two or three years. Collin will live at McKinley during the school year, as most of the other students do. Somehow they'll work out the money part.

As they leave, Matt catches his son looking over the other kids, their clothes, the way they walk along the paths, lie on the grass. Not alone. Not most of them anyway. "I'll start packing tonight," he says.

By the time Matt gets back to his desk that afternoon, the unusual joy that has buoyed him on his drive back into town is flagging. He sits down, glances at his blinking phone, at the messages piled in the basket in front of him. A throat-tightening sensation seeps through him. He tries breathing, deep, through his nose. But one can't breathe away sadness.

He found that out as he heard a doctor diagnose a son whose fingers tapped, arms flew as if he wanted to fly. Now, that same son is leaving. He would never have guessed, all those years ago, how painful this leaving will be. He reaches for the phone, will call his mother, but he doesn't. They'll talk Sunday evening after they've watched Collin hang up his clothes in his new room and he has waved them good-bye.

"You have to contact her," Grace says. "She's his mother. She has to step up to her financial responsibilities, if nothing else, after all this time."

"I don't know where she is." Matt has spent the day talking with administrators at Collin's old high school and in the school district office. They've told him that they believe his public-school education with special-ed support is sufficient. They will not recommend his going to a private boarding school, a recommendation that would mean the school district would have to pay the tuition.

This evening, he pours through his investment files, investigates online the possibility of Medicaid help, pencils out the amount of money he can get by closing out his insurance policies. He calls a friend who knows about second mortgages. Nothing worth pursuing. He can make the first-term payment. After that, it's a crapshoot. Whatever he ends up doing, it will wipe out any hope of a sufficient retirement account, even college for Collin. Maybe he could take a night job, a watchman somewhere. Some of his friends had done it in emergencies. He can't imagine it.

"You're a detective. Prove it."

"Grace, I don't think I can. I haven't spoken to Marge in ten years. She's chosen to become someone other than Collin's mother. I don't know who she is now, even if I could find her."

"Once a mother, always a mother. Believe me, I know." Grace looks away; her face closes, flooded in a visible wave of grief. "I still miss her, your sister." Her hands cover her moist eyes; she breathes, five breaths, through her nose, and she is herself again. "I have always felt responsible for her dying, you know. Your father tried to rope her in, keep her under his thumb, but I thought she needed to explore a little, make decisions on her own, not because of someone else's decree. Especially the decree of a man who drank until he hated the world. Maybe that's why I let her go out. To escape. Instead she died."

"When did you learn to breathe like that?"

"You taught me. Remember? A long time ago when you were becoming who you are today, a fine man and a good cop." Grace manages a small curve of her lips. "I'm sorry. I don't go back there very often and neither should you. Go find Marge. Tell her what her son needs."

"You've reached the Grahams." Matt recognizes Marge's recorded voice and takes a moment before he leaves his message. He doesn't want to seem demanding or pathetic. The subject is Collin's welfare, not his own discomfort at talking to this woman for the first time in ten years. "Hello, Marge. This is Matt. I'm calling to ask your help. Give me a call when you are able to talk."

He sounded okay, he thinks. Businesslike. He isn't quite ready when the phone rings five minutes later and it is Marge. "Thanks for calling back. I appreciate it." Way too formal. "I'm having a problem" No, not *I*. "Actually, Collin is having a problem right now, and the solution . . . "

"Problem?"

"He's being bullied—you know, the way kids do when someone's different. But he's done really well up to now—good grades, he's . . ." Matt wants to say *almost normal*, but instead he says, "he's been doing okay in school, once the therapy took hold. Actually, he's a pretty good kid, Marge. I'm proud of him."

A silence follows his last words. Then, "What do you need from me?" He remembers the voice, but her words have unfamiliar sharp edges that make Matt wince.

She's still empty of love, despite what Grace says about mothers. He tries again. "Not me—Collin. He needs to finish out high school at McKinley Academy, an alternative school for kids like him who march by a different drummer. He doesn't deserve to be miserable when who he is . . ." Matt can't come up with a word. Not *special*. Not *wounded*. Not *strange*. "Who he is, himself, is a good kid. A kid I love."

Again, silence. Then, "How much?"

Besides love for her son, she's empty of everything that Matt fell in love with years ago. Her clipped sentences, her impatience to get to the end of this conversation reveal a stranger, one with a rich husband, two stepchildren who visit once a month, and, according to his sources, a slew of real estate deals in the best part of the city.

Doesn't matter. "I can come up with ten thousand a year. The tuition is twenty-five thousand dollars."

"For about two years, right?" She seems to be making a note; paper rattles at the other end of the line. "I'm glad to hear things are going well for Collin. And, I hope, for you. Let me know where to send the check."

Matt has to ask. "Why haven't you called him?"

Matt can hear the inhalation on the other end of the line. Exhalation. She breathes, too. "I failed, Matt. I can't stand facing the child I failed." The line goes dead.

Perhaps Grace is right. Once a mother, always a mother, even one who believes she's failed. Especially, maybe, a mother who believes she's failed.

CHAPTER TWENTY-ONE

SARAH

SEPTEMBER 2009

When the noises stop scraping out of my aching throat, Ellie lifts the quilt from my face, and she leans close to me and whispers, "Don't say a word . . . about anything."

She doesn't have to tell me that. The minute I saw Rick's hand, I understood that someone I knew had done that to him, maybe Mouse or Leaky or, I couldn't stand to think of it, maybe Jimmy, sweet Jimmy, who's never done anything bad in his life to anyone else.

"Let the cops solve this one. We need to stay out of it." Then she picks up the photo from the table and turns it toward me. "See this? My son. Ten years ago he did something bad, maybe like one of your forest buddies last night. He was a wild kid, into drugs, like I told you, but not into much trouble, but this time him and a friend decided to mug some-one to get money to pay their dealer. The guy they robbed dropped dead of a heart attack an hour after they shoved a knife at his chest. I read about it in the newspaper the next day.

"The victim couldn't describe his attackers, except that they were white and young, but he said the weapon was an ivory-handled hunting knife. When I read about the knife, I went into the kitchen, opened a drawer, and I knew. The only thing Dan-ny's father had forgotten when he snuck out was his Primus hunting knife. I had kept it for twenty years—used to touch it once in a while to remind myself how young and stupid I'd been. It was gone."

Ellie puts down the picture, shakes her head. The way the hurt is riding across her eyes, tighten-ing her mouth, I wonder if she's ever told this story before.

"So what did you do?"

"I figured that it wasn't murder; the guy had a bad heart. My son had to learn a lesson before he really got into trouble. I'd never forgive myself if that happened because I didn't stop him right then. I called the police. But Danny'd seen the paper, too, and had gotten high on something to give himself courage or to forget maybe. When I hung up the phone, he charged out of his bedroom and came at me, knocked me down, kicked the shit out of me. He said he hated me. I said he wasn't my son anymore."

Ellie's fingers rub hard on her eyelids, holding back, maybe trying to find tears. "I haven't seen him since." When she looks at me again, her eyes are red, dry.

"Not your fault, Ellie," I say.

"He'd still be here—or somewhere—if I hadn't called."

"But *you'd* know. And like you said, if something bad happened after that, you'd never forget you could have maybe stopped it."

I know about never forgetting, about nightmares, about wondering what I could have done to make things different for my mother, and for me. My bad dreams are fading a little, but there is a wad of guilt stuck right under my heart that will never go away. Why should it? I'm about to tell her about it, to maybe let her know I understand, when she sits up, straight-lipped, folds the quilt into the neat square she uses to lean against when she relaxes on the davenport.

"Some things need to get forgotten." She pats the quilt smooth and sets it down. "All this commotion will be over before you know it." The look she gives me says the conversation is over. She stands up and heads for the bathroom.

But it isn't, really. Not in my head. I keep thinking about the two people, people I knew, good people, who are dead. One might be the father of my maybe-baby. The other was a soft-spoken stranger who helped a vomiting girl like a friend would. I could tell the sergeant what I know or suspect about Rick, his missing finger, what I heard in the camp, but if I do, I'll get my friends into bad trouble. Who'd believe them, dirty runaways, beggars, druggies probably, kids who don't appreciate what they would have if they'd just straighten up. Why wouldn't people believe they were also capable of murder? And maybe they are, I realize, if they're afraid enough.

The only real family I've had for a long time is Leaky and Jimmy and Peter and Lila and Mouse. I cannot hurt them.

And when he left this afternoon, Sergeant Trommald said the police would be searching the park for evidence, maybe the forest trails if they needed to.

I can imagine it. One night the scraggy bushes around the campfire will burst with uniforms, guns maybe, Leaky crying, Lila saying, "Fuck." I can't think what Starkey will do. Smile, maybe, ask the cops to join them for dinner like a good father would do. He won't crack; one of the kids will. Then, who knows? Whatever comes next will have to be terrible.

The only thing I can do is sneak back to the camp, warn my friends, help them get away. I don't care what happens to Starkey. Maybe I can even make it happen to him if my family is safe.

So when Ellie comes back out of the bathroom, crosses her arms in front of her, and says I need to leave, that she can't deal with trouble when it gets too close, I tell her I understand. I tell her I'll go to Transitions, the teen center on Ninth Street, find out if at sixteen I am still eligible for foster care. I can take care of myself, I say.

"Good. That's my motto, too. Make sure you get to the medical bus," she adds, looking at my stomach. "You need to know pretty soon."

I don't tell her I already went and that I don't have the courage to use the pregnancy kit they gave me. I don't want to know. Yet. I thank her for her help, pack up the clothes she's lent me, slip into her old red sneakers, and, without knowing I'd do it, I kiss her cheek. Her hand goes up to where my lips have landed, and she says, "Good luck." Her mouth twitches a little like she might tear up, but since Ellie never cries, she turns her head and looks at the door. I open it, say good-bye to the dull brown apartment and the good gray lady who lives there.

CHAPTER TWENTY-TWO

MATT

SEPTEMBER 2009

"This looks bad," Shelly says as she hands Matt a note. "Same neighborhood as the boy under the leaves. Peter, right?"

Matt takes the paper, sees the address. Yes, a block south of the oak-lined street. Yesterday they learned Peter Stafford's name after a worried mother filed a missing person's report when her son stopped making his weekly calls to let her know he was okay. Mrs. Stafford said her son had taken off to see how the rest of the world lived before he started college. Judging by the scars on his back and violated body, he had.

"Dead man in the lobby. Beaten, it looks like. They need to identify him. Guess he's pretty badly messed up."

"What did I tell you? Murder. Right here at our home. Get some protection in here. This is no way to live."

The same old guy is yelling at him from the front door of the apartment house. "I seen you before, Mr. Policeman. What are you going to do about this?"

Matt pushes through the people circled around the officer and sees a body, twisted into a bizarre crawling pose, his face a mash of flesh and blood. A trail of blood from the front door indicates that the victim dragged himself into the building.

"Does this man live here?" he asks, realizing too late that the answer will be "Not anymore."

"Did he?" he corrects himself.

"Hard to tell," someone answers.

"Looks like Rick's coat," another voice offers.

Matt reaches into the overcoat's pockets, feels papers, pulls them out. Candy wrappers. And a pink receipt of some kind. The letterhead indicates it came from the Williams Medical Clinic. He can't read the date, but among the blurred carbon words he learns that a girl was treated for flu symptoms and released without their consent. The notation was written in full caps. Perhaps that's how the van avoided liability claims when clients wandered off after being given a pill or a toothbrush.

"Anyone know a girl who lives here, maybe with Rick?"

The dubious looks he gets let him know that the idea of Rick with a young girl is hard to think about. "Rick was . . . " a woman in the front row says, "kind of raw."

"And crazy," another adds.

"The woman in 306 has a teenage girl staying with her. I seen them in the elevator." The old man again. This time he might actually be helpful.

"306?"

"Yeah, I kind of know her. Had me to dinner one time. Ellie, I think."

Matt leaves the officer to stand over the bloody pile of man and wait for the examiner and climbs the stairs to the third floor. The door of 306 opens after he knocks twice. He almost knows this woman. He remembers her eyes, startling blue, even now, although she must be close to seventy. Then he remembers the son, the mother smelling of alcohol, holding her ribs, lying. Not this building, though. Another 1980's project just like it a few blocks away.

"Sergeant Trommald," he says.

The woman lets him in; the girl he's looking for steps out of the kitchen. He jots down the woman's name. Mrs. Ellie Miller. She introduces Sarah, and the three of them go down to the stairwell in the lobby where a moist carpet of blood has spread under the body.

"It's Rick," Sarah says, her voice choked into a shudder. Mrs. Miller nods. They both turn away, and Matt stops them as they ring for the elevator.

"How do you know?"

"He's wearing the earring I gave him, and his finger . . . " Matt sees the woman's hand tighten on Sarah's arm, and she doesn't continue.

"His finger?"

The words dissolve into a low moan. "Why did they do that to him?" She wipes her eyes. "Can we go? I can't stand this."

Matt sees what she is seeing. A finger has been severed from Rick's right hand.

"We've done what you wanted." Mrs. Miller, her grip still on the girl's arm, turns them both as the elevator doors open. "Good-bye, Sergeant Trouble."

As they disappear into the elevator, Matt asks the superintendent to unlock the door of the small, windowless room this Rick lived in.

"Place is illegal," the super says, switching on a light. "But I felt sorry for the guy. He was sweet, you know. Always a smile under that beard, unless he wasn't feeling good. Which didn't happen so often, only maybe once every three months. Not like some of the sickos around here, permanently crazy, don't take their meds. One guy started camping under a tree in our back yard, what we call a yard, mostly Dumpsters, and scared the living daylight out of the garbage guys, claiming he had a machete, he'd kill them. Took three phone calls to you guys to get him out of here."

The super's guilt about the room has him trying to divert attention. "That so?" Matt says, looking at the sad life in front of him. A cot, a two-burner stove, a couple of bowls and a plate, neatly stacked on a table over which a calendar marked with *X*'s hangs. A photo of a young woman, graduation, big hair from the '70's, is propped next to a lamp on a chest. Matt opens the drawers and finds some T- shirts and underwear in one, and in the other, scissors, a harmonica, a couple of well-read books, and a notebook, empty except for the addresses and phone numbers of three people.

He copies the telephone numbers and leaves the notebook for the forensics crew who will be coming in after the medical examiner.

"Toilet's down the hall," he's told when he opens the one door in the room and finds only a couple of jackets inside.

"What do I do with all this stuff?" The super is whining.

"I'll make some calls. Maybe one of these contacts will want to look it over."

"Yeah, but . . ." Matt guesses that the man is worried. The quicker the better to get rid of the evidence of illegal rental. He's probably pocketed the rent without reporting it to the city, which owns the building.

"After the crew leaves, just bag it all. I'll let you know if someone wants it."

Back at his desk, Matt tries the phone numbers. The first number, California, is disconnected.

The second is answered quickly. "Williams Mobile Clinic, Jesse speaking." When Jesse learns that Rick is dead, she makes a little cry and says, "Not Rick! He was doing so well. He visited us just yesterday."

Matt tells her a few details and asks if Rick hung out with anyone she knew, someone who might have been with him yesterday.

"Everyone knows Rick," she answers. "He brings street people who need us to the van, and spends time talking with folks about their problems. Sometimes he plays his harmonica in the park, to take in a little cash, but mostly, he says, to give a little pleasure to others."

"Drink?

"He says he allows himself one beer a day . . . sorry, allowed. I can't believe this. That anyone would hurt this man."

A woman answers the third call, a long-distance number on the eastern side of the state. Laura Boyce, Rick's sister. "I've been looking for him for a long time." Rick left her home several years before after a terrible schizophrenic event, violent, frightening. She told him he should come back to her when he got back on his medication. He never returned. "I've been expecting a phone call like this. He was a good brother, really, but I couldn't have him screaming and crazy with my kids here." Her voice cracks and she clears her throat. "How did he die? Did you have to shoot him?"

Matt is not surprised by her question. The local papers have described in detail several police shootings of mentally ill men during the past summer. The supposed incompetence of policemen is good copy during the slow, warm months. Their competence rarely makes the front pages.

"No, Mrs. Boyce. Rick was murdered. But I do know from several of his friends"—he thinks of Jesse and the old woman and the crying girl—"that Rick was well-liked and has been living a stable life. We don't know what happened."

He has his suspicions, of course. *Crazy* is the word that some people use when they describe Rick. Someone else is crazy, too—really crazy. The boy, Peter, was beaten, stabbed, left out on the street. Rick was beaten, and judging by the amount of blood, probably stabbed, his heart and a stub of a finger sending out a red stream until he died in the lobby of the apartment house. Someone with a knife may be out there right now, walking the neighborhood, sitting on the bench in the park, waiting for more instructions from his personal demon.

Forensics can verify that hunch. Knives leave prints, as do objects used to beat in someone's brains.

Matt glances at his watch. He's missed it, Collin's graduation from McKinley Academy. Grace and Ben are at the school, and this evening they will bring his son home to Matt's apartment, and they will celebrate not only his graduation but his acceptance to a college located in town, one that specializes in computer technology.

Matt needs to do some grocery shopping.

"I'm not here," he calls to Shelly.

"Gotcha," she answers. "And congratulations, Dad."

CHAPTER TWENTY-THREE

JEFF

2004-2006

Two days after the visit from Fred's wife, Jeff sells his furniture to the guy who will take over the lease on the apartment. With a little money in his pocket, Jeff and his backpack head out to the streets. It has become clear to him that a hustling lifestyle isn't going anywhere. Without Fred and Danny dragging him down, he is free to look around, see what's out there. He is only twenty-two, with lots of time ahead of him.

He sleeps outside that first night, under sweet-smelling Doug fir boughs, combs his hair in the washroom of the park, slides the Northwest Acting School brochures in his pocket, and goes by bus to the school. He's on his way, he tells himself as he smiles at his reflection in the glass doors of the building.

The visit is disappointing. The receptionist—a student at the school, he guesses because of her perfect diction—informs him that he's missed the beginning of the term. She opens a folder and shows him the papers inside. "We have a waiting list of people who have auditioned and interviewed. Most of these won't be able to attend until next fall."

He doesn't want to give up that easily. He leans over her desk, reaches a hand toward her. "Perhaps you can give me an application and information on the kinds of classes I might expect. And the tuition?" His Grandpa Jack diction matches hers, and she gives him a slight smile as she opens a drawer and finds a folder.

"Good luck," she says as he walks away.

On the sidewalk outside, he searches the sheets of paper for the cost: $3,000 per term. That is that. He needs to earn a lot of money if he is to follow that dream, and hustling will not cover both the tuition and his need to eat and sleep somewhere. He is hungry. His shirt itches from last night's fir needles. *Fuck.* He hides his backpack in an alley and goes out to the corner to wait for a slowing car, a meeting of eyes. After a half hour of no action, a thought interrupts his attempt to keep an inviting eyebrow lifted. A wave of nausea moves through him. He recognizes the feeling, the same as he felt when he accused Grandpa Jack of using him, ruining him. And here he is, waiting once again for someone to choose him. No, not him, his body, a body that no longer is an enticing sixteen, even when offered like a dessert on a tray in a skintight designer shirt. He stays on the corner another half hour, being eyed and passed over. Then he decides.

The next day Jeff goes to the public library and enrolls in an online GED course. After three weeks and $250, the last of his cash, he takes the four tests and passes three of them. A week later, he takes the fourth, mathematics, again, and passes it too. The piece of paper he holds in his hand will be his ticket to a new life.

During his weeks of creating his future, Jeff has been camping in a park high on a hill overlooking the city. The day after receiving his GED certificate, he heads down to the street to look at the classifieds, find out what looks good, job-wise. He doesn't find it among the ads for auto mechanics and wastewater plant trainees. Back in the park, trying to figure out where else to go, the computer in the library, perhaps, he almost misses the kid rolled up in a ball under a bush. At first he thinks he is dead, but a jab with his foot brings a "Don't," and Jeff sees that the boy is crying, the tears smudging his dirty cheeks like bruises.

"What's up, buddy?" he asks, mostly out of curiosity. The kid looks about thirteen, but he says he is a little older. He wants to talk and Jeff listens. His story is familiar. He was kicked out of his house by a father who socked him in the stomach after he walked in on a scene in the TV room involving his son, another boy, and a hastily zipped pair of jeans. The other boy escaped, leaving his jacket behind, which is probably still under the couch. His father isn't much of a housekeeper, he adds.

"Your mom?"

"I don't know. She's probably glad I'm gone so she and Dad won't fight so much." By now, the two of them are behind a local restaurant, poking through day-old bakery stuff left out for anyone who wants it. The way Richard eats, ripping apart the bag of dinner rolls, Jeff can see it has been a while.

"Where are you staying?"

Richard chews, his eyes darting here and there, looking for more. "I don't know. Got kicked out of the doorway. They even took my blanket." He gets up, bent over like an old man, scuffles away without looking back. Something about the kid. The eyes.

Reminds him of someone. Without thinking why, Jeff catches up with him.

"Camp out with me," he says. "I got a good spot in the woods. Safe. And I got this," he adds as he pulls up his jacket and shows the knife hanging in its holder from his belt. "No problems."

The kid slides in next to him on the path, glances at the ivory handle, says, "Okay."

By the end of that week, three boys and two girls have joined them, and Jeff is teaching them how to live off the land. A gaggle of street kids is not in his plan, and no GED is required for this job, but he finds it strangely satisfying. Serendipity, Grandpa Jack would have said.

Jeff has never been looked at the way they look at him when he is talking. They listen, accept his rules. They go out and bring back food and a little panhandled money every day. They talk in the evening. Running the camp comes easy, like he's always known how, and Jeff begins to see himself as a kind of parent. He refers to the motley collection of orphans as his family. At first they laugh when he suggests he will be their father. But when one of the boys breaks the rule about burying his shit to keep the camp clean, Jeff takes a belt to him. That ends any question about who is in charge.

Jeff sets up a tent and a camp chair from Goodwill to emphasize his role. The others sleep wrapped in blankets from rescue missions that they fold and stack neatly when the mornings lighten their tree-shadowed camp. The group holds together for a month or so. Then Ronnie, the newest family member, doesn't come back one night after foraging for food.

"I said I wouldn't tell," Arrow says when Jeff asks him where Ronnie is. Jeff grabs his arm and yanks. Then he twists the thin arm a bit more and the boy screeches. "I think he went with someone, like, in a car," he whispers.

One of his grandfather's teaching moments, Jeff realizes. He calls his family together. "Prostituting is dangerous. Not only for you, but for all of us, your family. Kids on the streets selling themselves attract the police. If they find out where our camp is, we're done for. We need to stay safe." Safety is the goal of his fatherhood, Jeff tells them. And safety includes, he adds, the rule that sex among the family members must be consensual and protected, so no one gets hurt.

"That's one of the reasons I use these," he says to the gay kid that night in his tent as he unrolls a condom. "So no one gets hurt." This is okay with Richard.

The family makes it through the winter. They sleep under tarp-tents held up by nylon ropes tied to trunks and bushes at the edge of the camp. They learn to dig trenches around these tents to drain the water away from their sleeping bags and to keep scavenged wood dry beside their blankets. Local agencies hand out gloves and coats, and most of the family, including Jeff, eat at the mission dining halls whenever they can get in.

As the days lengthen and warm, and the trees and bushes in the park at the center of the town pop buds and a few blossoms, everyone leaves camp early, coming back to share food and stories around the fire in the evening.

Sitting on sunny park benches on the good days makes Jeff glad to be alive. He has an acquaintance or two he has a beer with once in a while, but mostly he likes watching the tourists walk by, discovering the mountains hiding in the clouds on the other side of the river, observing the buses full of commuters twice a day. He can't imagine working in these moments, except as something he might try when he is tired of playing father to six wigged-out teenagers. *Not for a while,* he thinks. *The GED will always be there.*

He has been reading an old newspaper left on his favorite bench long enough for two other loungers to come and go, and is about to head back to the camp when he notices a man, hands in pockets, sauntering along the sidewalk at the edge of the park, half a block away. The man pauses, looks back in the direction of the shop-lined street, waiting for someone, and soon a young woman in an open parka and a toothy smile runs toward him, her arms open. "I thought I'd lost you!" she calls as she wraps herself around him and they both laugh. He kisses her on the forehead, and it is his voice that Jeff recognizes. Danny, Danny saying, "Never ever. Best friends forever."

Danny, clear-eyed and happy, in love, living somewhere here in Green River. With a new best friend.

"Fuck you," Jeff says, getting up, feeling for the lump of weed he has been saving for an important occasion.

It is probably the good weather, unusual for this area in April. Jeff's little family has begun to get feisty about the rules, disrespectful, edging away.

The belt isn't a threat for a couple of them who've done belts their entire lives. Chores, the digging of the latrine, especially, get lost in the busyness of the languid days of early summer. "Heading out for San Francisco," Richard says, his backpack stuffed with the bread he's gathered this morning. "You've been great," he adds which makes Jeff angry enough to mutter, "Up yours," to which Richard answers, "That was okay, too."

One night only two strays, not really family members, join Jeff at the campfire. Alone later in his chair in front his tent, he drinks a warm beer and understands it is time to take out that GED and get on with his life.

Time to test your mettle, Grandpa Jack whispers.

"I'm ready," Jeff answers out loud as he throws the empty bottle into the dying fire. The next morning he packs up his clothes and heads to the day center where he takes a shower, cuts his hair and shaves with the razor he's discovered in the inside pocket of his backpack.

After spending a day in the library looking over first the jobs online and then the *ASVAB for Dummies,* he walks into the army recruiting office and takes the test. He does okay, good enough to get the recruiting sergeant's eyes blinking. In a month or so, he is in boot camp, in a camo uniform and a shaved head.

He knows the decision to join the army has something to do with the day he watched Danny being hugged in Pioneer Square by a woman carrying a bag of vegetables. Jeff has never been hugged like that, and he hasn't shopped for a head of lettuce or anything else for a long time. Not that the Army will offer either of these moments. It will, though, bring a future that doesn't involve a camp in a forest.

CHAPTER TWENTYFOUR

ELLIE

SEPTEMBER 2009

I like the quiet. I've got nothing to agitate me except maybe the Stephanie Plum mystery lying open on my bed. After I make my morning coffee, I sit in the fake-leather chair and check the calendar. Wednesday, graffiti day. Why not? I've been inside for two days. Time to get back on track.

My bag of supplies is waiting in the coat closet. My apron, too, and I see when I walk down the stairs to the first floor that Rick's grocery cart is still tucked under the steps. Efficient as he is, even having managed the cleaning out of Rick's room, the super has missed the cart and its bags of cans and bottles. One of these days someone will be happy to discover the estate of a good, crazy, dead man.

Gray day. I'm moving slow, spraying without enthusiasm, rubbing with a weak wrist. I catch myself looking over my shoulder for a girl with raccoon eyes. But it's good she's gone, safe somewhere, I say, probably out loud. A home, maybe, a new life.

Who am I kidding? It's not that good for me that she's gone. I was getting used to her and her wet towels on the bathroom floor. If things had gone differently, if she had just stayed with me and maybe gone back to school and had let her hair go brown or back to black, but not both, if . . . *Stop*, I tell myself, pressing hard on that silver paint that never comes off easy. Thinking of ifs doesn't do anyone any good. Time to begin forgetting, like I told Sarah.

The first blue mailbox is covered with scribbles that look like ancient alphabets. Can any of these taggers actually read this stuff? Maybe they've come up with a language no one can decipher except other delinquents.

I am thinking about this as I come up to the next box. Something new here: not hearts or organs or scribbles, just an orange smiley face inside a circle, a diagonal line crossing it out, like a NO PARKING sign. A NO SMILING sign? The orange is different, too, a pen line like the silver I hate, narrow, hard to get off. I take out my scratch pad, push against the metal, mutter a curse word or two until I've dislodged most of it.

Someone is standing behind me, watching. Another old man. This time a long white beard waggles at me. "You get paid for doing this?" I don't bother to answer, just pick up my bag and move on. I find another crossed-out smiley face on the next box and get rid of most of it before I head back to my apartment. I've got some turkey soup in the freezer. It's probably still good.

At the knock, I open the door. I don't know who I'm expecting, but it isn't a policeman, the same one from a few days ago.

"I don't think you remember me," he says.

"Of course I do. Sergeant Trouble, wasn't it?" *What now?*

"Trommald." He steps in, like he did before, notebook in hand. "We also met a few years ago. You called the graffiti office, complained that except for you, no one was doing anything about it around here. You said that it was driving you nuts, the vandalism in your neighborhood. Could someone help?"

It's coming back to me. I was using some dumbshit stuff I bought at the paint store to clean up, and because I didn't know what I was doing, I removed a little paint from a couple of apartment building walls. Some of the old buildings in my neighborhood are maroon underneath their modern gray coats, and my efforts left ugly bruises. The manager of one of them came out and told me to stop making his building look even worse than the graffiti jerks.

I realized I could get in trouble for the same kind of crime that I was trying to do something about, and I needed to find out the rules of cleaning up. The cop who came by told me that the office would supply the Graffiti X. Public objects, okay, but not the red STOP signs because they lose their reflectiveness; private buildings have to take care of the mess themselves, or the city will for a price, usually leaving behind a patch that has nothing to do with the color of the building's paint.

I learned all this from the policeman who is standing in front of me at this very moment.

"How's your son doing?" he asks out of nowhere.

"None of your business," I answer.

"Sorry. I was also remembering the problem you two had about ten years ago. I came by your old apartment after your call to the station. I was a patrolman; probably you don't remember me. I felt sorry for you and for him, especially you. But you seem to be doing okay," he adds, looking around my brown living room.

"And all I remember about you is your *Graffiti Hurts Us All* button. Is bothering old ladies a comedown or a promotion?" But he's right. We've had conversations three times. The first time when Danny left me twitching against the doorjamb. I moved from that place to this one, and then it was Rick dead in the lobby. And once, sometime in between, he's reminding me now, I called the graffiti office for advice.

He smiles a toothy smile, then relaxes it when I don't respond. "The truth," he says, "is that I had a kind of bad spell for awhile. I was reprimanded for doing something stupid and ended up working the graffiti squad for a few months."

"Yeah? What?"

He raises a hand to his forehead and rubs a frown away. "I was drinking," he says, "a lot," and he looks at me like he knows I'll understand. Probably because he's seen me drunk, sunk against a wall. "I asked a fellow officer to show me her thong. My then-wife didn't wear one, never would. I was curious, in an innocent way."

"Sure. And?"

"I got demoted to graffiti, for one thing." He gives me a better smile, meets my eyes, his hazel, honest. "I'm in homicide now. Not drinking, only mildly interested in women's underwear."

"And you're back to talking to me."

"And I'm back to investigating graffiti, and you're the neighborhood expert." He looks toward the davenport, and I lead him to it.

"Instant?" I ask, and when he nods, I go set the pot on the burner.

Sergeant Trommald is forty-five-ish, good-looking in a pouches-under-the-eyes way, a look that makes you think he's gone through a lot and has come out the other side scarred but maybe wiser. The hand he takes his mug with doesn't have a ring on it. I imagine he's seen a few other undergarments since then. He's capable of getting the juices running even in an old lady. "So?" I say in order to interrupt this futile line of thinking.

"What I'm going to tell you is restricted information, Mrs. Miller."

"Ellie," I say. A girl can dream, can't she?

"Another body has shown up. On the play equipment in the park, a teenager, no identification except for an ID card that turned out to be fake. He was beaten and stabbed to death, like the other two victims."

I try to keep my face still, but inside my guts are turning upside down. Which kid I almost know from

Sarah's stories has gotten it this time? I hope not Jimmy. Sweet Jimmy, she called him. "Shit. What's going on?" My next thought is how glad I am that Sarah is safe someplace far away from the forest. Maybe she'll never hear about this kid on the playground equipment.

"We managed to identify him from a tattoo and a birthmark as a runaway from Snohomish. He apparently had been in town only about a week or so. Where you come in is what he had in his backpack. Two paint pens, the kind that go on in thin lines. Artists use them, and kids who tag. Like on mailboxes, traffic signs. Orange."

"Orange?"

"You've seen some around here."

"Crossed-out smiley faces. Just today. First time I've seen orange. I Graffiti X'd them. Sorry, Sergeant Trommald. I wiped away the evidence." *Sarah's safe.*

"Matt," he says. "And it's okay. We have a theory. Not about the orange graffiti, exactly, but about the murders. Three transients—your friend Rick excepted, maybe, because he actually had a closet to sleep in—three transients are murdered, left to be found in or near the neighborhood park down the street. The only connection between them, other than their homelessness, is the murder weapons, a rounded instrument. Maybe a baseball bat. And a knife, a hunting knife, we believe."

I'm imagining as he sits back and takes a swallow of his lukewarm coffee that he's wondering where I've hidden these weapons. I am so relieved about Sarah that I'm cracking jokes to myself. I hold my lips straight, serious.

"We're looking for these items," he says. "All over the neighborhood, including the shrubbery around the apartment buildings, the park's bushes, the edge of the county forest. We think that a transient, probably a mental case, is taking out his anger on folks who can't fight back, storing his equipment somewhere near. And we're wondering what message this kid was sending with his orange paint." He takes out his pad, writes something down. "Seems ominous, doesn't it, a crossed-out smile?"

I think of a girl whose street name is Smiley. She's gone from my apartment, from the sick little park. I'm thinking of the other kids out there under the trees, not safe and not innocent. I can't put them in more danger than they are in from all sides. I shrug, pick up our cups.

"Good luck," I say. "I wish I could help."

CHAPTER TWENTY-FIVE

JEFF

2006-2008

At first, he thought he'd probably been out of his mind to join the army. He hated the torture of the unceasing physical training. He dreamed of slashing the brutish red face and simian lips of his sergeant with the butt of the weapon he was supposed to be learning to use. He made no effort to talk to the one-syllable-word ignoramuses who slept and ate next to him. He'd made a terrible mistake.

Then, a month later, he sees himself in a mirror as he shaves, admires his rounding pecs and his tanned skin and realizes he's never been in such good shape. Except for the haircut. He's changing physically, and maybe in other ways. This military experience may be not only a means of getting out of a tent in a forest, but, even more important, a chance to take back some control of himself, of his life. He's the smartest guy in the platoon. He can do this. Jeff forces himself to listen, obey, and volunteer, and even smile once in a while. He manages to get himself chosen as platoon leader before the end of two months, a model soldier.

When he is asked which career he wants to train for, he lists the administrative string of jobs that his test scores, especially the verbal ones, are good enough for. Journalist, broadcast journalist, intelligence analyst, counterintelligence agent. Any one of these will be okay. He has learned he can follow someone else's rules when necessary, especially when he considers the paid tuition to the college he'll choose when he walks away into his next life. He is pleased when he is sent to a communication school in Arlington.

However, the nighttime anxiety that has rattled his sleep since he was a little kid still visits him as he buries his head under a pillow to still the groans and mutterings of his fellow bunkmates. Unbidden fragments pass across his closed eyes. Danny's laugh, an old man's fingers, the back of a father's hand, a mother's red lips, the flick of a knife, Kitten's soft brown boobs . . . the shards come together, dissipate, a constantly moving kaleidoscope until the Ambien takes hold. In the morning, Jeff cannot remember the patterns, only the vague sense of loss that accompanies them.

The broadcast journalism classes are a perfect fit. He likes himself on camera. The army has chiseled his cheekbones, hardened his body. His hair, grown out a little now, is cut in the precise way he wore it when he hustled. He has the voice and the words, and after a few months, he has appeared on the military television channel enough to make a small name for himself.

After a particularly successful interview of a female colonel on sexual harassment in the service, he is asked to lead a committee of fellow students working to partner with PBS. At their first meeting, as they sit and drink coffee, Jeff looks around the table and sees the others nod at him with respect, admiration, even, and knows he is on his way. In the end, their efforts don't amount to much, but Jeff revels in the role of leader, as he always has.

And he makes a friend, the first real friend he's had since Danny. Xavier is younger by a couple of years, street-smart, and like Jeff, ready to change the direction his life has been taking, which has included getting mixed up for a while in an L.A. gang war and watching a brother get shot down in front of the neighborhood mercado.

The two of them share where they have come from, and they share their dreams of where they are going. Jeff can imagine himself reading the news on television. Xavier is a writer and wants to report from the midst of the action. "Maybe in Iraq," he says, his brown eyes wide, excited. "Or Somalia. Somewhere far away." They spend free time on weekends drinking beer, laughing, and sometimes talking about the grit of their pasts, especially when they have had a beer or two too many.

"Do you have a girlfriend? You never talk of one," Xavier asks one night between mouthfuls of a burger. Up to this moment, for almost two years of friendship, Jeff has managed to derail this subject with a raunchy joke or a yell at the game on the TV above the bar.

"Not really."

Jeff looks over Xavier's head at the college basketball game. "Did you see that? Foul, I guess! Terrible ref."

In this new life, he's packed away thoughts of sex like a box of old photos he doesn't want to look at for a long time: his past profession; his dalliances in the woods; his grandfather; and, at the bottom of the box, his disinterest in women, a disinterest, almost a revulsion, in fact, that he can't deny anymore as he listens to the moans of men jacking off to Playboy pin-ups behind the doors of the toilet cubicles. His own self-pleasuring is silent, drowned in the midst of a sea of midnight snores, his fantasy sometimes involving an amorphous young boy. Himself, maybe, he thinks more than once, as he stirs and then falls asleep. He finds this kind of relief as necessary for sleep as Ambien.

"Haven't found the right girl," he says, when he sees that Xavier is not distracted by the game. He swirls the beer in its paper cup, waiting for whatever will come next.

"Me neither." Xavier keeps chewing, wipes his mouth with a wadded napkin and tosses it across the table. "No right girl."

A door opens and Jeff steps through it. "Or the right boy, maybe?"

Xavier shakes his head. "When I was about thirteen, I had a crush on a kid and I thought I was gay. Scared the hell out of me. Beat him up." He laughs. "Felt good, and I kept beating up people for the fun of it."

"What was he like, this kid?"

"Tall, smart, popular. Didn't know I existed until I shoved him into a locker after PE and almost broke his jaw. He said I was crazy, and I guess I was. Dale Whitman. Still remember his name."

Jeff raises his cup, remembering. "Yeah. Like Danny. Long time ago. Except I knew what I was scared of." He swallows the last of his beer and wills himself to continue, a test. "My grandfather introduced me to that kind of sex—buggery, he used to call it, joking. He's dead, but not before he'd trained me to be his baby ho." A panicky heartbeat propels his alcohol-loosened words. He closes his eyes, leans back. Waits.

Xavier shifts, takes a French fry from Jeff's basket, doesn't get up as Jeff expects him to. "I heard of stuff like that," he says. "How'd you come out so normal?"

Jeff breathes, is able to laugh. "They say marijuana is medicinal," he answers. "I took a lot of medicine." He almost touches Xavier's hand as it reaches for another French fry. "Here. They're all yours," he says instead, pushing the basket toward his friend.

A month later they finish the final phase of their course, and rumors indicate that the graduates might be sent to any one of the American Forces Network locations outside the United States. Jeff and Xavier join a few other classmates in a celebratory tour of pubs and watering holes, and when the others go on to seek whatever other entertainment they can find, the two friends start walking back to the base. The possibility of being separated is sad, they both admit. The two street kids have come this far, and who knows when they'll get back together.

"Facebook," Xavier says woozily. He leans against a wall, his eyes closed under a palm. "Waiting for a moment of clarity," he adds. "Hang on for a second. Might vomit. Lotsa beer tonight."

Jeff eases the hand away from the closed eyes, holds it. Another hand held his like this long ago. He cannot stop what is about to happen. "Before all this is over," he whispers, his words slurred, warm, "you need to know that I want you, Xavier." He moves closer, presses his erect penis against Xavier's thigh and for a moment, neither of them moves. Then Jeff feels the sting of the slap, hears the word, sees Xavier plunging away from him.

"Faggot!" his friend yells. The word sounds like a sob.

An orderly delivers the commander's letter three days later. It confirms that a general discharge is mandatory when homosexual behavior is reported. A witness, a fellow soldier on his way back to base, corroborated Xavier's report. Jeff signs the receipt of the notification and chooses not to seek counsel.

He does not see Xavier before he packs his bags and walks away from his army career.

He works his way back toward the West Coast, hitch-hiking, and by bus when the rides are hard to come by. His less-than-honorable-discharge papers mean that he is ineligible for the GI Bill, so he won't be going to school when he arrives in Green River. Somewhere in Wyoming he decides to use his small savings to buy another tent. He'll go back to the woods and plan his next move. One thing for sure: there will be no more Dannies and no more Xaviers in his life. Friendship, like love, is a figment of a 3:00 A.M. imagination.

CHAPTER TWENTY-SIX

SARAH

SEPTEMBER 2009

I'm not going to Transitions, of course, or to the social-services office a few blocks away. I'm heading into the forest.

But first I have to have a plan. I head to the homeless youth shelter I hate. I can stand one or two nights there while I figure out what I'm going to do and get a couple of meals.

Except for the screaming nightmare one of my roommates has, the center turns out to be a good place to think. The counselor says, "No pressure," when I say I need a little time to get myself together before I talk to her, and I spend most of the time pretending to read magazines in the lounge.

All I need to do, I decide, is get close to the camp and when the kids come trailing in for dinner, stop a couple of them and tell them they need to leave, that the police are looking for them. *Pass the word,* I'll say. I won't need to get near Starkey.

First, though, I have to find the camp. At breakfast the second morning, I sneak a couple of rolls and an orange into my duffel. I'm ready.

To reach the family, I have to go around the playground, cross the soccer field, and push into the bushes that separate the city park from the paths of the county forest that lies like a green blanket over the hills overlooking the city. I've never done this alone. Peter and the others knew where the camp was, and I always followed them.

The county forest is crisscrossed with marked trails, signs pointing one way or another, mileage noted ever so often. If you look closely, though, other paths lead away from the groomed trails and cut through underbrush and over rocky mounds. All kinds of people use these unofficial trails to get into secret parts of the forest.

A year ago a family was discovered living in tents and growing vegetables and storing hazelnuts for the winter in a secluded but sunny spot tucked against a hillside. A dog off-leash followed his nose and interrupted their berry-soup meal. The parents and two kids had been there a year, had gone down for library books every week, panhandled for stuff they couldn't grow or make, saved rainwater in an abandoned water tower. No one had stumbled across their camp in the whole time they lived there—the woods are that dense.

And sometimes hikers heading off-trail get lost a half-mile from the three-story houses at the edge of the forest and make the headlines. At least, that's what Starkey warned as he taught us to live off the land and the Dumpsters below us.

An hour later, I leave the marked trail and am stumbling through the undergrowth when I see a path nearly invisible under ferns and low-lying bushes. I follow it to a beaten-down patch of grass covered with beer cans and cigarette butts. A few condoms wilt in the debris. I turn around, leaving the love nest to the people who created it.

I keep heading up, zigzagging between rocks and mounds of bushes and tree trunks that are handy to grab when I slip in the soft mush of the forest floor. The sun is edging against the tree line, shadows beginning to narrow the path, when I spot a couple of birch trees that look familiar, see an ax cut on one, a marker of some kind. I am scratched and itchy, probably covered with poison oak since some of those bushes look familiar. Maybe Starkey warned us about them, too.

I drop my duffel under a tree root and sit down on a rock. I take off my jacket. Not poison oak, I discover. A couple of spiders have had dinner on my arms. For a minute I wonder if I'm some kind of magnet for bad things, from poisonous spiders to everyone I love dying. Not everyone. Not yet. I stop scratching, take out the orange, and look around.

From my low angle, I can see, through the ferns, a foot-wide trail heading straight up, cutting a track in the underbrush. I think I remember this path. I toss the orange peels and get up, stoop low, try to step quietly despite the ankle-twisting rocks hidden under moss and debris. In minutes, my hair drips sweat on my neck and my hands sting from scratches. I don't remember getting to the camp being so hard. I haven't found another mark on a tree. Then I spot a couple of deer hoof prints in front of me.

Shit. I'm following an animal trail. And I've left my duffel more than an hour behind me. I'm about to turn around when I feel as if someone is close by, watching. I stop and moving only my eyes, glance through the tree trunks. Nothing. Then I look up and laugh. A wooden water tower, most of its boards broken and hanging, leans like an old drunk against a couple of firs at the top of the hill I've been climbing. Probably the one that family used. No danger here, unless I get too close to it and get bopped by a falling board. I keep going.

The sun's disappearing behind the hill when I see a wisp of smoke floating like a gray ghost above the trees. I follow it and come to the edge of the camp. It's almost time to eat. The kids will be trailing in with their Dumpster offerings and icy thirty-two-ounce tubs of drinks bought with panhandled coins downtown. I'll wait for them out under the trees. But where is Starkey?

Sounds lead me toward a patch of grass still bright with sunlight where I see him lying naked, working his penis. His back is arched, and his chest heaves with moans that come out of his stretched mouth like curses, his fingers frantic. His heels have dug into bare dirt, the grass under them beaten down. I watch for a minute, but then I remember why I'm here.

I slip back into the woods and sit down next to a tree trunk. I'm tired; my whole body aches. I wake up to Leaky leaning over me, shaking my shoulder.

"Hey, Smiley! You're here!" Before I can answer, Jimmy and a couple of new kids I don't know wander up, and I don't have time to tell them to shut up. Jimmy pulls me up and drags me to the fire ring. "Look who we found," he calls.

Starkey is sitting in his throne chair. He has his clothes on. His cheeks above his trimmed beard are no longer wet with sweat.

"Welcome back," he says.

CHAPTER TWENTY-SEVEN

JEFF

2008

Things have not changed much in Green River. Homeless kids still sit around with their dogs and packs in doorways and on corners, telling stories, asking for money, using, getting kicked out of shelters when they won't quit and learn to do something productive. They need more than a shelter. They need a family, a realization that Jeff came to on a bus somewhere in Idaho as he stared out the window and considered his future, as hazy as the mountains on the other side of the steamy glass.

It won't be difficult to bring another family together, to lay down the rules, instruct, and protect a few of them from the dangers of the street. He'll offer safety, like a good father should.

Seven street kids accept his offer.

After the first few weeks, Jeff understands that his talent for parenting, the discipline coming so naturally, is enhanced by a thread of cruelty that weaves through his relationship with his children. His willingness to hurt when the hurt brings obedience no longer surprises him, a trait maybe learned facedown on a carpet from his father or in a breeze of uplifted blankets. Or, more likely, he thinks, in boot camp, where grown men wept. Whatever—it works.

Like the evening his knife slashes a boy's face when he laughs at something Jeff has said during a lesson on trust. Just one slice, a permanent lesson etched on a smooth cheek. A week later a twist of Cherry's red hair encourages a screech and a confession to holding back a couple packs of cigarettes from the family. As a reward for her truthfulness, he hands her a hank of her hair and she takes it, whimpering, "I'm sorry." A tip of a forefinger lands on the last piece of pizza as its hand reaches out for it, bloodying but not spoiling the cheesy triangle.

"All part of building loyalty," he assures his campers. "All necessary in building our new family." They look at him. "Understand?" They nod, their wary eyes not quite meeting the sweep of his glance as it moves across them.

One night, after a powerful evening's fireside chat on fathers that leaves a couple members with wet eyes, Jeff is revved up, full of energy, at odds with the quiet scene he's created. He needs something more. He looks at the still-teary Scarecrow, a waspish boy in donated clothes that are so big he could have pulled himself into them and disappear, and, despite a warning heartbeat or two, he invites him into his tent. The others send jealous, narrow looks in their direction. Jeff smiles, enjoying an unexpected sense of power this envy gives him. He closes the tent flaps, Scarecrow in hand. However, when Scarecrow understands what is about to happen, he begins to cry, choking back sobs, screeching "no" more than once.

The next morning, lying alone in the tent, Jeff knows he's made a mistake. Outside he hears the little wimp whispering to someone that he is leaving. He says he can't do what Jeff wants him to do, no matter what. Jeff gets up, walks out down the trail to think, comes back to the usual slow exodus of kids from camp, knows how he will save his family.

By the end of the day when everyone comes back from town, Scarecrow is not among them, although his blanket roll is still shoved under nearby blackberry canes. Jeff thinks it best not to dwell on the empty spot at the fire, telling the others that Scarecrow has made a choice to leave and now he has to live with it.

Except, according to the *Times* Starkey picks up a week later, Scarecrow's bled-out body has been found in a roadside ditch, a knife having pierced his spleen and then for good measure, his heart. The family speculates about rumors they've heard on the street but since they don't read newspapers, they continue to make guesses about their friend's disappearance. Jeff, to bring closure to the fireside gossip, gives a short eulogy one night before dinner as he announces the boy's death. He reminds them again that Scarecrow left the safety of the family, and look what happened.

Then he tosses Scarecrow's blanket roll in the fire pit and, as he smells the acrid burning wool, feels cleansed, as if he's appeased an angry entity.

Camp life continues quite calmly into the next winter, a few hungry kids wandering in and leaving after a meal, the core family of five or so thirteen and fourteen-year olds remaining. Each night Jeff delivers what he calls his homilies as they sit cross-legged around the fire, a captive audience. The winter has been unusually rainy and cold, and he knows that his charges, young and afraid, don't have the guts to leave their tarp-and-cardboard homes and go out on their own.

Sometimes Jeff wonders if, as in this forest family, it is fear, not love, that holds most families together. Certainly true for him with his father and grandfather. Maybe Danny, too.

Sunshine, a new girl, remains in camp after her traveling partner moves on to look for her boyfriend in town. Sunshine likes listening to Jeff. She grins when she hears him say something she wants to believe, like when he says that God is inside all of us, not out there somewhere like an all-seeing video camera. Since God is inside us, we can decide what God wants of us, which means, really, that as long as we are loyal to each other, truthful, we can do whatever we need or want to do.

Jeff has begun to think a lot about God, about spiritual ideas, about rules for living a good life. Sometimes he wonders if the thoughts come from somewhere, from someone else, channeled through him to instruct his family, the way the words flow. He enjoys the admiration he sees in Sunshine's eyes, the respect she offers when she applauds his words.

After a few weeks of such sermons, one night Sunshine crawls through the door of Jeff's tent, opens her down jacket, and presents her naked self.

"This is what God wants for me," she says, kneeling and reaching for Jeff's crotch.

An hour or so later, the girl heavy in his arms as he carries her down a trail, Jeff decides that Sunshine's biggest mistake was not the girlish giggles that erupted as she touched his penis lying limp and small as a dead smelt after she finally got his pants unzipped. Her error was that she believed the voice whispering to her was God. Had she doubted for a short moment that God wanted her to crawl into his tent—a ludicrous idea since God probably knows how Jeff feels about women—she'd still be alive, perhaps screwing the kid with the pimples who stared at her through the flares of the fire.

So, after his early-morning delivery of her tarp-wrapped body to the other side of the park, Jeff takes his time meandering along the tracks and the small paths that will bring him back to the camp. He considers the situation. Children aren't allowed to laugh at their parents, are they?

Jeff is quite sure he didn't laugh at his grandfather's reluctant penis. Even if he did, this is different. The old man had only his ego to worry about. Jeff, however, is certain that Sunshine's laughter has destroyed everything he's worked so hard to build in his family, the respect he's seen in their eyes, the loyalty he's created, the control he wields over his willful children. He has done the right thing, getting rid of her.

What he needs to do now is re-establish his role as a father. A new kind of discipline. Higher expectations, more difficult chores, perhaps. He needs to be more paternal.

However, when his finger brushes against the still-damp red stain on his jacket sleeve, a whirl of nausea spins in the pit of his stomach. He's gone too far this time. One of the kids may have seen him leave with her. Probably did. It was still dark, and he didn't think to be quiet. He leans against an overhanging rock, tries to plan. He must leave before they have a chance to talk to each other. He will hurry back now, call the family together while they are only stirring in their blankets, not awake yet, explain that he's been called to another city to help others in the way he's helped them. He will give the camp to them, he'll say, a place to live as a family like he has taught them. Yes.

He needn't have worried about the good-bye speech. When he gets back to camp, everyone, everything is gone. All the packs, all the portable food, even the matches to light the fire.

Everyone except dimwitted Alfred, who is on his knees in front of Jeff's tent, scratching a wobbly *Fuck*

You into the mud. He looks up, says, "Oh, Oh," the last words Jeff allows him to utter before he uses his knife one more time. He wraps Alfred in the only item his family has left behind, bloody and of no use to anyone. His sleeping bag.

Jeff buries the boy in the latrine trench and heads south. Green River has been unlucky, always. Not that his hometown contains any portion of himself anymore, but its streets are familiar, its buildings less imposing, and its parks more hospitable. He knows a few people in that town, people who owe him from the old days, and he knows the huge county forest. The five traitors in this family, free to talk about what they suspect and have seen, will be two hundred miles away.

For the time being, until he makes sure he isn't on anyone's radar, he'll disappear into the trees of McLaughlin.

CHAPTER TWENTY-EIGHT

MATT

SEPTEMBER 2009

In one of those quiet moments that bloom in the midst of conversations, Matt glances at his son and grins back at the smiling face across the table.

"What?" Collin asks, wiping his lips with his napkin. Cloth, because this is a special celebration.

"Nothing. Just feeling good," Matt answers. Grace and Ben nod in agreement. They are all feeling good. Their boy is home for the summer, is headed for college, is almost grown up. His new car, actually an old VW, is parked in the driveway, waiting for him to take it out for a spin, maybe to his friend John's house a little later on.

Who would have imagined it, ten years ago? Beyond good, Matt can't give a name to his feelings at this moment. Sad, relieved, grateful, hopeful, and perhaps a bit lost. What else? Ready? For whatever is next?

However, later that evening, the dishes cleared and leftover pasta saved for tomorrow's lunch, Matt is not ready for the phone call.

"Matt, it's Marge."

"Marge." They haven't talked since she sent the last check nine months ago. "How are you?"

"Good, mostly. I'd like to talk to you, maybe over coffee? Sometime soon?"

Her voice is calm, her words' sharp edges wrapped in silk, urgent.

"Something wrong?"

"Not wrong, really. I'd just like to . . . I want to get to know Collin. I'm not sure how to go about it. I need to know how he feels about me, whether he'd be open to me inviting him over, meeting me on my territory. Now that he's older . . ."

Cured, she means. Matt feels his chest do its tightening thing. He breathes a few times.

"You know, able to relate to others better, I thought he might enjoy getting to know his other family. Can you and I meet, talk about how to do this?"

Matt imagines her hand on her BlackBerry, ready to record a reminder of time and date. "No," he answers. "I'm not participating in your reconciliation with your recovered son. That's your job. Perhaps it will happen, but without me. Your son talks on the phone. He can drive to a coffee date, if he wishes. It's pretty much up to you, Marge."

"You sound angry."

Good, because he is. "By the way, Marge, you need to know that Collin is not your normal college student yet. He still taps his fingers when he's anxious. And he gets anxious a lot. He still doesn't read others' faces well. He still has problems with intimacy, and when he likes a girl, he embarrasses himself and her with what he says to her. He will be continuing therapy and training into his adulthood." Matt pauses. He could go on, but he probably doesn't need to. "Do you really want to introduce him to your new family?"

"You're an ass, Matt. I'm sorry I even thought to call."

"Maybe you're right, but I'm also a father. And I, too, am sorry you called."

He doesn't get to sleep after that conversation. Has he robbed Collin of a chance to get to know his mother? Somewhere around midnight, he decides that his first instincts were correct. This is Marge's problem, not his. About the same time, he hears the

VW pull into the driveway and the front door open quietly. He falls asleep.

At his desk the next morning, he revisits his conversation with Mrs. Miller about the orange graffiti, the dead boy. She was holding back something, something that made her sagging chin raise up like a feisty guard dog's when he mentioned the crossed-out smiley faces. And where is the girl—Sarah, her name is? Not in the kitchen this time.

A fax comes in from forensics. The weapons appear to be the same in all three murders. A rounded wooden bat, a six-inch knife. It seems to be a confirmation. They are looking for a serial killer. Perhaps the crews out scouring the park and the edges of the forest will find something, a hiding place for either the weapons or the lunatic using them. He'll hear if they uncover anything useful.

Until then, he'll shuffle the papers spilling out of his IN basket.

Just before noon he hears voices at the office door. Shellie leads a well-dressed couple to his desk.

"Mr. and Mrs. Crandall," she says. "Sergeant Trommald."

For a moment, Matt doesn't recognize these people. When the man speaks, though, his deep bass voice is familiar. It is the same voice Matt heard when he called Snohomish to tell them of their son's death. The kid on the play structure.

He shakes their hands. "I'm sorry for your loss." He gestures to the two chairs across from his desk.

The couple sits, Mrs. Crandall looking at her husband, waiting for him to speak. When he doesn't, she says, "We have to know how our son died and why. He was only fourteen. Jeremy was a good boy." She pulls out a crumpled hankie from her pocket. "He ran away because he heard us quarreling, because he couldn't stand the thought of his family changing anymore than it already has."

Her husband licks his upper lip, continues their story. "His sister died this year. Leukemia. Her death hit us all hard. Maybe he thought everything was . . ."

"Falling apart. And now it has." Mrs. Crandall wraps her arms around herself. Her thin frame presses against the back of her chair.

Her husband reaches for her; she shakes his hand off. "We need to know," he says, "so we can . . ."

"Find some peace." She allows him to touch her shoulder. They both wipe tears away with their free hands.

Matt cannot think of what to say. What words can console these sad people? Perhaps there is no consolation until the pain and guilt dissolve into a ragged scar they will carry for the rest of their days, part of who they are.

"Your son was killed by someone we now believe is a predator, preying on people who seem to be homeless. Jeremy was not homeless. He had a loving father and mother. He would have headed home, I'm sure, once he understood that despite the problems there, it was the place he belonged."

"He called us once. He said he was okay, staying in a camp of some sort where they called him Sampson, for some reason. He said he was coming back soon." Mrs. Crandall's head raised, her voice a little stronger.

"He knew you wanted him home. He wanted to be home, too." That phone call may have killed the kid. No reason to mention that.

"Who did this?" Mr. Crandall was back in control.

"We don't know, but we are working very hard to find him. We'll let you know when we do. In the meantime, can you remember the date and time of your son's call?

CHAPTER TWENTY-NINE

JEFF

SEPTEMBER 2009

O nce he has the new camp laid out—a tent as usual, a fire pit and the beginnings of a latrine—Jeff decides to create a new persona for himself. His name will be Starkey, a name he remembers from a book he read in the third grade about a pirate. The idea of a theme amuses him. He trims his beard into neat dark whiskers. A mustache blooms on his upper lip. A kerchief tied around his head, shades, and a gold earring complete the look.

And, as important, he's made a new personal rule. No more sex. Sex erodes power. He began to understand this as he traveled from Green River to McLaughlin, following a coastline whose trails led him far away from towns and people possibly looking for him. A difficult trip, but the silent walk through forests and along surging waters offered hours to reflect on his life to date. So many times he'd come close to real power, to meeting whatever goal he'd set for himself. In every case, sex had led to failure. A high-class prostitution business financed by wealthy clients like Fred, the army and college dreams, plans with Danny for expensive homes and travel, even his families of children who offered him control over their lives. Perhaps he regretted those failed families the most. His power over them had been the purest sort, intimate, as if he were connected to them and they to him in every aspect of their lives. Fatherhood suited him perfectly. However, sex had destroyed each family, sent his children flying away like sparks from a dying fire.

By the time he arrived in McLaughlin, found a good spot for a camp, he understood that he was going to try one more time. This time he would not fail.

Starkey stretches out his legs and settles back into the old canvas chair in front of his tent. He likes his new self, a daily reminder that he has become a different, more self-confident person. The evolution has taken a few years, and a few bad scenes, but now he's feeling very competent in his role as father to his new McLaughlin family. Not that he intends to be a pirate/father/tent-dweller forever. No, the skills he is honing at this forest camp will lead to a much, much better place.

He has a dream that emerges in the peace of moments like this. He can imagine a life in which he becomes wealthy while protecting, grooming, and profiting from a stable of thirteen-year-olds. Not a stable, of course. A home, filled with antiques and good rugs. Gracious. Comfortable rooms for the men who will pay well to be serviced by clean, healthy young boys. Several of his sons in this new family would probably be eager to be taken care of this way. Despite his new rule about sex, he still has fond memories of the compliant, even eager, Richard. He'll multiply that scene by twenty, all participants' needs met in a safe and pleasant way. All he requires is a backer to get started.

He rubs his rough chin. Time to get out the scissors. Appearance is half of this father job. The other half, of course, is letting the family know who's in charge.

The first months in McLaughlin, he didn't need to discipline very often. Perhaps it was the knife, a totem at the fireside or on his hip. An old bat, one of the kids found on a playground, helped, too. Later, when a few family members questioned his authority, the bat became a notched scepter, leaning against the canvas throne at the back of the fire, a fresh slice in its handle each time it was swung against a body part of a recalcitrant son or daughter. A ritual bloomed.

Ritual is an important part of getting this job right, Starkey has discovered.

When a family member sloughs off orders to find firewood, collect food, clean the camp, for whatever reason, Starkey requires that the group, assembled in the evening around the fire, help with the discipline. He often picks the most innocuous kid, maybe the one who still sucks his thumb when he sleeps, to take the bat and swing it against the guilty brother or sister. "Again," he commands if the halfhearted swing doesn't result in a body thrown sideways or to the ground. The knife comes out, a groove is carved in the handle of the bat, and Starkey compliments the batter for helping the family. Like a good father does.

Then Peter brought a new girl to the camp—Peter, tall and wiry, a soft-spoken man-boy about whom Starkey had doubts from the beginning. When told of his initiation task, also a ritual, Peter dared to ask why he and Jimmy needed to carry weapons on a midnight mission.

"Loyalty to our family," Starkey answered, touching the knife at his side with his fingertips. "Your job is to find someone who needs beating up. You'll use our bat." Peter was not unfamiliar with violence. Starkey had seen the scars on Peter's back, still angry red, carved there by someone the boy would not talk about even in the most intimate evening sharing times. Peter hesitated, picked up the bat, nodded to Jimmy, and headed out of camp down the hill. They returned with a bloody weapon and this hooligan girl who calls herself Smiley.

Smiley has lived up to her name. Firesides begin with Starkey's sermons and end with Smiley's laughter, until the night Peter lands in the fire, after being disciplined for his inattention to the lesson. The circle breaks apart. Some move to help Peter get up; others turn, look toward their bedrolls. Starkey calls everyone back to the fire. "You need to know why I'm so tough on you," he says, and then he tells them about his tough early years. Some of his family can relate to his stories, have had grandpas and cousins, even mothers, with Grandpa Jack's proclivities. They hesitantly tell their stories, too, and the shared secrets calm the circle. Despite Starkey's original annoyance at the change of atmosphere as they gather each evening, the family seems stronger than it has ever been. The bat isn't used for several weeks.

Gradually, though, Starkey becomes uneasy. One night, watching Peter and Smiley sit in the center of a noisy cluster of kids, he senses a subtle shift of leadership. He realizes he needs to put down the coup developing in front of his very eyes.

In the past he has given the family members loyalty tasks: graffiti messages, stealing specific items from grocery shelves, roughing up midnight campers under the bridge, but this situation calls for something more.

"I believe," he begins, the flames of the fire lighting the ten sets of eyes in front of him. "I believe that we are getting soft, losing our raison d'être, losing the glue," he goes on to explain, "that has held us together over past months. We need a challenge, a task that will bring us to a new level of understanding as to what this family is all about."

He pauses, focuses his gaze on the boy and girl holding hands at one side of the circle. "Two of you will be required to help rid the community of its living detritus. Useless debris," he explains. "Perhaps the homeless turd who sprawls in an alcoholic swoon across a sidewalk in midday. The schizo who refuses to take his meds, screaming at the teeter-totter that is attacking him. The meth-scarred ho lying on the park bench, her children not even memories."

Starkey can tell by their stillness that he's gotten their attention. "It is time for our family to be a force in the community, not a complacent nodule." He isn't sure about that last word, but he does know what he is going to say next. "Two of you will be chosen to bring back the finger of a person without whom society will be better off."

He stands up, picks up the bat and the knife, waves them toward his family, and slips through the flaps of the tent pleased with himself. If he is ever grateful for anything about Grandpa Jack, it is the pile of words the old man stuffed into him that surfaces at moments like this.

When he wakes up the next morning, he sees that Smiley's place next to Peter is empty, her duffel gone. Peter is kneeling, stuffing his sleeping bag into his backpack.

"I'm going, too," he says. "You can't stop me." He stands up, and when Starkey steps toward him, Peter swings a fist, catches an earringed ear with a hard-knuckled blow. That's when Starkey picks up the bat and uses it on the boy until he crumples, the family watching, a couple boys yelling "Stop!" but not intervening.

"This is what happens to a traitor," Starkey says, breathing hard, taking the knife out of its holder. He was too soft on this kid from the beginning. Should have eliminated him one way or another a long time ago. Now all he can do is show the others that Peter, and, in turn, they, will not get away with disloyalty to the family.

It is over in minutes. Peter is wrapped in a ground cloth, his pockets emptied, a wallet searched for money, as Starkey has instructed. The silent kids crouch near the fire or bury themselves in their sleeping bags. No one leaves the camp all day. That night he and a trembling Mouse, who asks, "Are you sure?" until Starkey tells him to shut up, deliver Peter's body to a pile of leaves near the park.

CHAPTER THIRTY

2

ELLIE

SEPTEMBER 2009

I wake up the next day to doors opening and closing, hallway speculations, people in uniforms pushing aside plantings and shoving aside garbage cans under my window. The park is cleared of fall leaf droppings, the beds neater than they've ever been in my memory. All along the forest boundary, machines roar through and cut back the branches and blackberry canes overhanging the narrow road, rakes poke here and there, their tines tracking neat patterns that will last until the next rain. The third murder hasn't made the newspapers, although the gossip in the hallway gnaws on its possible details.

"Some crazy person out there. They don't want to get us stirred up," my old-man dinner partner, Mr. Levitz, surmises as we stand in our slippers on the front steps. "We'd be marching on city hall if we knew for sure."

Sure, I think. The only thing that has gotten this neighborhood of tired, sick old people marching was last year when someone said that our new president would try to kill us all off. The march itself almost killed off a couple of us. You can go only so far with a walker. Then someone mentioned that we'd all die sooner or later, and until then Medicare seemed to be working, so why worry? It was a relief to be able to go out of the building without someone grabbing your sleeve and trying to slip a flyer in your pocket.

By now most of us are back into our routines, waiting for the lunchtime volunteers with their Styrofoam boxes, complaining about the heat in the radiators, the slippery leaves on the sidewalks.

Except I'm not. The last few nights, sometime around three in the morning, I've woken up and gone over all the details. Not of the murders. Of my life. Conversations slink in, fill my mind with words and sick feelings, then evaporate, leaving behind eyes that won't close and pains in my stomach. I turn over, try to get back to sleep, and instead move on to the next scene, not in time, but following some winding trail of guilt: the morning I raise a fist as I stomp out of the room, screaming, "Why did I ever have you?" to a cringing three-year-old.

And later, when I try one more time to be loved, I get "I never loved you, ever," instead. The man laughs and shakes his head as he throws the suitcase filled with his clothes over his shoulder. He stops at the doorway. His face goes mean as he turns to me. "Especially not now. Look at you, drunk, as usual."

"Look at you, you pervert," I yell back as he disappears into the stairwell. I feel good, freed up for a second, no more worries about always having to please someone else. Then I hear Danny bawling in the next room.

The other times. The night I notice and don't care about the dirty fingernails of the guy I am picking up at Murphy's, focusing only on the bills in the wallet held by those fingers. The day I wake up to Danny pushing my head against a vomit-crusted pillow. He is crying, and as he hands me a damp washcloth, he says, "I thought you were dead." He is about nine, quiet and bringing home bad report cards.

"We're alone, just the two of us," I excuse him to his teacher. "It's hard on both of us." The teacher looks at me, wrinkles her nose at my whiskey breath, and answers, "I can see that. Maybe the school counselor, Ms. Williams, can help," meaning the both of us, but I never call the woman. I can do it myself, I am sure.

I really did believe I could do it myself, back then when I swam through a river of bourbon each day. My midnight mind scuttles over the drunken scenes barely slowing down, there are so many of them. Danny moves in and out of those years, cooking beans and wieners sometimes, disappearing for days, coming back to yell at me and me at him. I threaten to kick him out one day if he doesn't go to school. I'm sick and tired of the school calling me at work; I'll lose my job, I say, and he laughs at me.

But the worst times, the last times, the ones that make my mind freeze shut, begin the night I grab his jacket, pull out the baggie holding the white crystals, know he is either dealing or using, probably both. I screech at him, spilling out all the anger the bourbon has churned up and kept splashing inside me for ten years, how I hated the man who walked out on us, how Danny is just like him—lazy, stupid, going to jail, how I have to work in a pit of a laundry in order to feed him and how he . . . In my almost sleep, the words still pour out, hot behind my eyelids, and they are so full of poison I have to sit up and turn on the light to stop them.

But when I lie back down, Danny's face reappears. We are fighting at the door of our apartment. Now he is the poisonous one. He has heard me call the police, report him as a possible accomplice to a robbery I've just read about in the newspaper. "How could you? I'm your son. What kind of fucking mother narcs on her son?" His face is wet with tears, and he wipes his eyes with his palm.

Then I see the fist coming my way. It lands on my shoulder. I hit back, brushing his chin. His next jab sends me to the floor. A Nike comes at me. I feel a shot of pain in my ribs. I hear Danny say, not yelling, leaning down over me so close his words feel hot on my cheek, "Fuck you, Mom. Someday I'll pay you back for this goddamn life. You just wait." He slams the door of his room. I can hear drawers being pulled out, him cussing.

When I push myself upright, my ribs hurt like hell and I am angry, and all I can think of is to call 911. I might need a doctor. I make my way toward the door and the phone down the hall, but someone is knocking. I let a policeman in and lean against the doorframe, barely able to talk. When he hears the officer's voice, Danny, stone-faced and dry-eyed, comes into the living room. He just shakes his head as I tell about his hitting me, about this son who needs to be taken in hand, straightened out. "Juvie, maybe," I say, "before he decides to really kill me."

Danny lets himself be patted down, and the cop doesn't come up with anything, but he opens his notepad, looks around the apartment, and I realize later, probably takes in the bottle on the table, the glass beside it, the smell of neglect and dirty dishes in the sink, the smell, in fact, of me. He writes it all down, asks about the robbery I called about.

I look at Danny. His pale face, stiff with hate, makes me say I've made a mistake about the call; I was mad at my son, and I admit that's what started this whole thing.

The policeman looks at both of us, decides we're through going at each other, says I should call if we have any more problems. He hands me his card and leaves. A minute later Danny picks up his suitcase and follows the uniform out the door, and, except for one call from my son and instructions years later about graffiti removal, I don't hear from either one of them again.

Until this week. Sergeant Matt Trommald drops in during the day, and my son, Danny, visits me every night.

CHAPTER THIRTY-ONE

JEFF

SEPTEMBER 2009

After the Peter incident, Mouse, who usually lives up to his name, shows signs of not being willing to pick up the ceremonial bat, the use of which comes into play more often as family members slack off on duties.

Then Lila comes back to camp talking about seeing Smiley sitting with an old guy with a gray beard on a bench and her going with him. Starkey recognizes an opportunity to reinforce his demand for loyalty and to initiate two of the new members, Bebop and Jasper, into the ways of the family. "No one helps a traitor to this family," he explains, the two boys nodding open-mouthed. They've been told about Peter.

That night, Starkey hikes down into the park with them. They find the old gray-bearded guy on a bench, drinking a beer, singing, and after the boys use the bat, Starkey finishes the job with the knife. Then he hands the bloody knife to Jasper and points to the limp right hand at their feet. In a minute or two, a bloody finger is tucked in Bebop's fanny bag. When they hear footsteps nearby, they slip away into the forest.

A day or two later, Starkey reads that the old guy was able to crawl away to his cave somewhere to die. Not a problem, since he wasn't talking when he was found.

It is strange, he thinks, reviewing recent events as he lounges in the camp chair beside a dwindling morning fire. Some of the family members are very willing to accept the family's need for order. Jasper and Bebop, for instance. They carried out their chore without complaining.

However, others—like that mama's boy Sampson who'd joined the family last week—thought they could get around the rules, trying, as Sampson did yesterday, to sneak a call home. Peter, of course, was the worst offender, attacking his father, bringing violence to the family circle. Some kids are just born weak or bad, Starkey thinks. Nothing a parent can do to change them.

Now that he understands the rules of fatherhood, he is confident that this particular family, despite a few disruptions, in this liberal town, in this receptive forest with its paths to the nearby city Dumpsters and sympathetic pedestrians with change in their pockets, this family is going to be the best one yet.

He does have to do something about Smiley, of course. She is the only one to run away and not be disciplined. That is a concern.

The sun feels good on his face. He turns toward it, takes off his sunglasses, and shuts his eyes. He has never felt so relaxed, unencumbered with doubt. He gives his crotch a squeeze, decides he'll nap instead, while the sun is still warm.

Moments later, he hears rustling on the path. Sitting up, he sees a tall man in dreads and a beard wandering around the edge of the camp. "I'm real hungry," he mumbles when he notices Starkey. "Any extra food? I've been traveling for a couple of days."

The two men look at each other, Starkey in his kerchief and whiskers, the other with his matted hair and beard and muddy jeans, and after an astonished moment, they grab at each other and hold on.

"Call me Starkey," Jeff tells Danny once they sit down over a couple cans of beer. "Remember that book we read when we were about nine?" Danny doesn't. "Pirates. I needed to change a few things about myself, including my name."

"You look good," Danny says. He brushes at his stained thighs. "I should clean up."

"Later. Let's catch up. Why did you come back?"

Over the next hour, Starkey learns that months before, Danny left the woman he once thought loved him. He ended up on the street, so depressed he wondered if he'd be able to lift his feet to find his next meal. He slept on benches in the park and under the freeways where the police, under the new Green River Council Clean Parks Initiative, hassled the camps until it was hard to get a night's sleep anywhere.

Starkey opens another can of beer. "I've been there," he says. "Fuckin' police. It's better here in McLaughlin."

Danny shrugs. "After getting beat up a couple of times by kids looking for drugs, I decided to head back to this town. I haven't a clue whether my mother is still here." He swallows the last of his beer. "And I don't care."

Jeff knows Danny must be remembering their last fight, the apartment, Fred, the easy money. Skipping the part about Fred and his wife, he brags a little about joining the army, getting trained in journalism, which turned out to be a dead end, his decision to help homeless kids up north. Now he is working down here in the trees he and Danny ran to that first time. "Social work. I'm good with kids," he says, feeling how right on these words are. "They respect me. Especially kids who need a father figure. You'll be surprised."

"You've always been someone people looked up to, gathered around." Smiling his familiar smile, Danny adds, "Remember our times smoking shit in that first apartment up there? You could have led those kids right off a pier, they liked you so much." He shakes his head. "I guess I just didn't want to get led, especially by someone I was jealous of, even though I needed a father bad."

Starkey breathes in the unspoken apology, knows he can tell the rest of it, about the family he's built here. "Discipline. The infrastructure of strong families. And the rule enforcer, the father, always. Not the mother, as you well know." He pauses, allows himself a sigh. It is good talking to someone who understands. "In this project, of course, I've had a few kids who wouldn't follow our rules. For the benefit of the others, they learned what happens when they disobey. Most of the family is doing well, though. You'll see when they get back. I'm proud of what we have here."

It probably isn't the time yet to talk about the idea of the expensive house for the expensive kids.

Not really Danny's kind of business, but who knows? They open two more cans of beer, hold them up, and toast the moment, as they did a long time ago under the freeway, and Starkey feels something click, as if a broken connection has been repaired, a warm hum flowing between them once again.

"Here's to the new you, a pirate named Starkey." Danny's grin seems to mean that he feels it, too.

CHAPTER THIRTY-TWO

MATT

SEPTEMBER 2009

It is 2:00 PM when Matt returns to his desk from lunch. He looks over his emails, and among the numerous interoffice memos, he notices a fax from a Lieutenant Small, GRPD, entitled "Urgent."

The lieutenant, an officer in the Green River police department, informs him that an operative, an undercover agent, code name Seattle, is moving into the McLaughlin area. After learning of murders in Green River very similar to three reported in McLaughlin—homeless kids, same kind of MO—they have sent him down to find out what he can about a man who in Green River was known as Jeff, the name the kids in his camp in the woods above the city called him.

"We've just been notified that fingerprints from a beer can have identified this individual as originally from McLaughlin, one Jeffrey Moore, whose prints were logged in the U.S. Army files.

"We are quite sure he is responsible for at least three murders here. Researchers looking at your recent murders suggest he may be in McLaughlin. No known relatives. An informer describes Jeffrey Moore as about six feet tall, about thirty, dark eyes and hair, bearded, likes good clothes and haircuts, even though his home has been a tent in the woods, speaks as if he is educated.

"He gathered a cultish group of street kids, and they lived for a year or more in the woods at the edge of the city. He apparently controlled them with promises of safety and threats of punishment. The one teenager who agreed to talk about Jeffrey Moore says that he liked to call the kids his family, say he was their father, but one family member vanished while our informant lived in the camp. There are rumors of more disappearances among the family. The disappearances coincide with bodies found in or near the woods.

"Our agent Dan Miller, aka Seattle, will be in touch with you. Let's keep in contact."

Matt makes copies so that he can discuss the information with his team in the morning. A serial killer, probably psychotic, for sure very dangerous.

His desk is almost cleared when Grace's call comes in.

"Not to worry you, Matt, but I just got a call from Collin's therapist. Collin has fired her."

"Why, for God's sake?"

"He feels he doesn't need her any longer."

"What does she say?"

"Whether he's right or wrong, he has to try life on his own."

"What do you say?"

"I'm about as worried as I was the day you said the same thing to me."

"And?"

"You called me when you needed me."

So this is what it's like. Letting go of a child. It feels like the hardest thing of all, at this moment. "So, he'll call her, or us, if he needs to?"

"We'll find out, Matt. Let's go out to dinner tonight. This may be an important event in several of our lives. Ben says he's paying. He says we deserve a reward."

"Damn, Grace," Matt says as he hangs up.

The thing is, when you let go, you don't stop worrying. You just do it while biting your lip to keep from saying no.

For some reason, he thinks of the old woman, Ellie, what must have been her good-bye to her son.

At least Collin and he never tried to beat each other up, didn't leave each other bloody and angry. At least Collin and he will be talking to each other ten years from now. Maybe.

The phone rings. When he answers, a voice warbles at him, a poor cell connection. "I can't hear you," he says.

"Seattle reporting," the voice seems to be saying. "I'm in a camp at the top ridge of the county forest. I'm concerned about what's happening here. You . . . " The line goes dead.

Matt calls an emergency meeting of his team. It's time to start searching the forest beyond the park. For some reason, he remembers Ellie's last name, Miller. He looks again at the email. Seattle's real name is Dan Miller. Not possible. Lots of Millers in the world.

CHAPTER THIRTY-THREE

SARAH

SEPTEMBER 2009

"**W**hy are you back?"

Starkey aims his squinty gaze at me, and he's not smiling. The kids are sucking on their Slurpees, their worried eyes asking the same question.

"I thought I could make it alone," I said. "That's why I took off. I didn't want to keep following the family's rules. I wanted to make my own rules." I blink like I'm about to cry. Maybe I am. "I found out that I couldn't do it. I wasn't safe. I almost got beat up, and then I got really sick and I got hungry." I give Starkey a begging look. "I'm sorry I left. I want to be part of this family again."

Starkey raises his eyebrows as if he's astonished at the idea. "We'll discuss it tonight, after we do our chores and eat. For now, your job, Smiley, is to gather firewood. Like before." He waves a hand, and the drinks are set down and we all scatter. We all know that the sooner we get finished with our jobs, the sooner we eat. Starkey leans back in his chair, looks up at the sky with its faint dusting of stars.

When Jimmy crosses my wood-seeking path with his shovel—not a spoon now, I notice—I stop him. "Jimmy, the cops are looking for the family. They don't know it's us, of course, but they know someone is in the forest, killing people." I don't keep whispering because Jimmy is walking away, shaking his head. I pick up dead sticks until I have an armload, and I bring them back to the fire. Lila and Mouse are stirring a pot. They don't look up as I set my load down and say hi.

Then I see a bearded man sprawled on a log, watching us, his knitted cap trailing dreadlocks onto his shoulders. He's older than the rest of us. Shadowed valleys reach from his nose to the corners of his lips and lead to a scraggly beard that grows out of his neck as well as his cheeks. If it weren't for his eyes, blue and alert, I'd be afraid of him.

"Hello," I say. He nods but doesn't speak.

By the time we circle for dinner, I understand that I am getting the silent treatment from everyone, even though Leaky pats half of his sleeping bag for me to sit on, like he remembers how I used to share a pad with Peter. In between spoonfuls of stew, the kids talk in whispers. The new ones look at me, their eyes neither afraid nor uncaring, just curious. No one mentions Peter, and I know I'd better not, either.

Owl, the slow girl, collects our cups in a plastic bin and goes out to the creek to wash them. At Starkey's signal, we reach out to hold our brothers' and sisters' hands and wait for his evening lesson.

"A quiet moment to reflect on our blessings, food, a place to sleep, a family to take care of us." We bow heads; someone starts a hand squeeze and we pass it on. Then Starkey begins.

"The one element that makes a strong family different from any other grouping of people is loyalty. And loyalty is built by sharing tasks, secrets, and beliefs. In our family, we are very good at sharing the tasks of living. You are learning to open your hearts, reveal the secret parts of yourself, and not hold back anything—your past, your dreams, your fears. What you have shared in this circle is the intimacy that binds us together, gives us our strength, protects us from a world that doesn't give a shit about us. We know just about everything about each other, don't we?"

Heads nod, a few twitchy smiles. I am wondering where this is leading.

"And our loyalty gives us the strength to keep the truths of our family from the outside world, doesn't it?"

More nods. I am beginning to understand.

"And it is our belief that our family is the source of our courage. As your father, I have the family at the center of my every thought and action."

Starkey leans back now, looking at us, touching each of us with his gaze. "I am worried. I am sensing a questioning spirit floating in the air, doubts eating at the trust we have built up so carefully." The bodies on each side of me shift a little, eyes glancing around without any heads moving. A small, anxious breeze passes over us.

"By now, most of you are familiar with the idea of testing. We've talked about how Moses was tested on the mountain, just as Jesus was tested in the desert, just as Muhammad was tested by the hegira, each to prove his loyalty to his higher power. I've decided that each of you must be tested another time to prove your loyalty to our purpose."

Leaky is squirming, his foot jabbing against my hip. I wonder if it's a warning or a memory that is circling through him, making him tense.

"We've someone staying with us for a few days to watch how we live together, how we succeed as a family. As I told you last night, he is interested in us because, where he comes from, families like ours are falling apart, arguing, disappearing. Disloyalty has leaked information to the authorities; camps have been destroyed, children set adrift. I've known this man"—his hand drifts toward the bearded man next to him—"since we were younger than you."

The rest of the family has heard this speech before. They are nodding. This introduction is for my benefit. No one, including Starkey, will look directly at me. I glance at the stranger, and I know I've seen him before.

"He's asking that we call him Seattle, his street name. The two of us have had many adventures together. We've lived on the street together, and we have shared the secrets of our sad and hurtful lives as children with each other. After all these years, we are still loyal to each other, and that's why I wanted him to meet you, see how we do things."

Seattle raises his eyes to us; his glance lands on me and stays a fraction of a second longer than it does on the others, and he says, quietly, "I'm very impressed with you all. Thank you for letting me hang with you for a while."

Starkey moves on with his program for the evening. "First, we need to give Goose a hand for her contribution to our kitchen supplies. Five cans of beef stew, the food that fed us tonight." Everyone claps, and a skinny girl with stringy blond hair held down by a knitted surplus army cap looks down, pleased.

"And we know that Bebop and Jasper completed their loyalty task without a hitch, and we have the evidence to prove it." Starkey holds up a jar filled with liquid and a pickle. No. Not a pickle. A finger, white in a pink fluid.

"One less lost soul for the world to push around." Not Leaky and Jimmy, thank God. Bebop and Jasper must be the two black boys sitting on the other side of the fire, looking at each other, then at their boots, uncertain grins flickering across their lips. *Rick, Rick.*

"Unfortunately, one of our newer family members did not understand the importance of loyalty." Starkey gives Seattle a sad shrug. "He was found trying to phone out to the world, and I felt it necessary to discipline him. Sampson won't be back, and someone will have to take his place as a communicator."

Sampson was probably on graffiti patrol, his job to send out the word that we exist, that we're angry, that we survive despite how the world treats us. Maybe he was trying to get back to a lost mother, like Jimmy was with his *MOM* hearts. Maybe, I'm realizing, that's what most of us are trying to do: find our mothers. I don't hear Starkey's next words, see that everyone is looking at me.

"And are you missing Peter? No, Smiley, he's not here and you know why. When you left so abruptly, went back to the unwelcoming arms of the streets, Peter tried to follow you. But not before he committed an even worse error, that of challenging me." Starkey looks at Mouse and smiles. "We ended that disloyalty."

That's when I see the hunting knife in its leather case lying on the edge of the fire ring. I can imagine how it went that night, Peter rising up, Starkey swinging the bat, Mouse too afraid to do anything but whatever Starkey asked.

"We knew you'd want to see Peter again. You were good pals, right? So Mouse and I left him buried in leaves near the park Lila saw you in a few days ago."

With Rick. Maybe Rick's murder wasn't as random as the cop thought. Maybe it was meant to be a message to me. Like Peter under the leaves. Who will my body be a message for? The rest of the family? Anyone else having doubts?

CHAPTER THIRTYFOUR

ELLIE

SEPTEMBER 2009

I'm sick of remembering. Really sick. I've thrown up SpaghettiOs and lettuce, this week's offerings from the food bank, and now I'm getting rid of yesterday's Rice-A-Roni. Maybe I'm allergic to food past its due date, but old food never had this effect on me before. Even Perry Mason doesn't cure me. Or Sue Grafton. I decide to take a shower, clean up, both inside and out.

Sarah's left her shampoo, a sample-size bottle with just enough left in it to suds up my hair. It smells like Sarah. I could use her now, at my sickbed. I lift my leg over the edge of the tub, inhaling the last of her.

On the floor in between the sink and the bathtub, I see a plastic pill container, the one I took out of Sarah's purse days ago. The brown pills, four or five of them, rattle as I pick it up, look at the label again. This time I can read a few of the words. A telephone number, the last name of someone who bought the pills. And I can barely make out the small print at the bottom that says the pills are amitriptyline, or something close to that. Not my business.

But a half hour later, I'm calling the number on the label and a voice says, "Sellwood Pharmacy. This is Stella. May I help you?" I have to think fast.

"This is . . . " I look at the name on the label, "Mrs. Jansen?" I don't know why I made that a question, but I go on. "I have an old bottle of pills from you in my bathroom cabinet, and I'm wondering what they were for? And whether they are expired?"

"Do you have the prescription number?"

Damn. No number. "The bottle must have been in the sink, water or something. I can't read it, but I do have the name of the drug, and maybe you have records there of my buying it?"

"Name again?"

I say, "Jansen," and then add, "It's stupid of me to not remember why I got these, but I've been under stress for a while, and I'm finally feeling better." That sounds lame. "I do want to know how to dispose of whatever this is. I read in the newspaper the other day about the pollution of the river because of drugs being flushed down the toilet." I let that sink in while the woman is apparently looking up Jansen.

"Sorry, we store our records after five years. You're not in the computer. Not sure I can help. What was the name of the medication?"

I spell it, squinting at the small print, hoping I'm getting most of the letters.

She says to wait a moment, and when she comes back she tells me it is an antidepressant, probably expired, and it should be disposed of by putting it in a container of used coffee grounds and sent along with the garbage.

I thank her and hang up and go back to lie down on the davenport. I don't have coffee grounds. Not my problem. None of this is. So why am I lying here, eyes wide open, instead of sleeping off whatever is going on in my stomach?

Sarah Jansen? Why, more than five years ago, when she was still wishing for a Samantha Parkington doll, would she have been taking antidepressants? Maybe she stole these pills from someone. Why was she carrying around old pills instead of swallowing them? If she bought them on the street, wouldn't they be in a baggie or something unidentifiable? Was she selling them? Same question: why in the original pill container?

I go back to the hall and steal the phone book. Children's Services, I guess. State? County? I pick a number, jot it down, and go out to the phone.

When someone live finally answers, I say, "I am worried about a young girl, fifteen or so, who has"—what should I say that won't get her into trouble?—"stayed with me for a few days and has gone on to a relative's home. I am hoping she is off the streets right now, and safe, and I need to let someone know that I'm interested, maybe this relative."

"Is she one of our cases?"

"She said she was in foster homes until recently."

I give the woman the only name I have, Sarah Jansen. She comes back a few minutes later. "Yes, she has lived at several of our foster homes, in fact, until she ran away from the last one a few months ago. Her caseworker is very worried about her. Is she there with you now?"

"No, she's left and I haven't seen her for a while. I just thought that if that relative had her, I'd like to see her again, make sure she's all right." I make my voice sound old and harmless. "She is a beautiful young woman. I wish she was my granddaughter."

"Sarah apparently had no family left after her mother died." I can hear pages flipping in the background.

This is where I have to ask the right question. What is the right question? "She told me her mother died. Cancer, right?"

"I don't think so. Says here probable suicide." The woman hesitates, then adds, "I'm sorry. I'm way out of line." She's official again, says, "We are interested in Sarah being safe. If she shows up, please let us know, and tell her we are here to help her. Thank you for being concerned." She asks how they can contact me, and I give her Stella the pharmacy lady's name and number.

So now I know. I am holding in my hand the drug that killed Sarah's mother. The very last thing her mother touched, found by her daughter under the bed or between the mattress and the box springs. I put the vial in my top drawer, next to my underwear, where I also have hidden a locket that protects a browned, fading photo of a young woman, my own mother.

She died, too. I was five, and the last thing I remember of her was her hand waving at me from the train window as she left for the sanitarium. I never saw her again. They had orphanages in those days, not foster homes, and to keep me from going to such a place, my grandmother took me in. She fed me, taught me to be clean, and made me go to school. She sewed my dresses from printed flour sacks and checked for nits in my hair. She had worries of her own: a dead husband, her own four boys all hard to handle, heading into trouble or the army. She never held me, did not touch me except for the occasional swat. Once, she tried to teach me how to quilt and I blew her off. I didn't want to be mothered and that was good, because by then she didn't want to be a mother. A couple of years later, I escaped that house, scraped clean of love and heavy with despair, by getting pregnant.

And here I am, a sick old woman about to go to the toilet one more time. Only now, I feel better.

CHAPTER THIRTY-FIVE

SARAH

SEPTEMBER 2009

Starkey shifts in his chair, looks again around the circle as he reaches for the knife, takes it out of its case. "We searched for Smiley, didn't we? And here she is, back in our family. So handy." Leaky's foot has stopped bumping into my hip. No one is moving, maybe not even breathing. I try to speak, know I can say nothing that will change Starkey's plan. I hold my hands in my lap to keep them from shaking.

"Have you come back to be forgiven, Smiley? Or did our message on the mailboxes around the park scare you into thinking you could convince us of your loyalty to us?"

Mailboxes? I don't know what he is talking about. Doesn't matter. He keeps talking.

"Neither is possible. You'll stay with us a day or two and spend time regretting your decision to run away from us. Perhaps you've even told the police about our family. Lila says they've been all over the park and the neighborhood today. One officer even warned her about a crazy transient who they suspect has killed a couple of people. 'Be careful, young lady,' he said. 'Don't be alone in this park.' Lila says she laughed in his face."

Lila's dark eyes deny that statement. They are wide with fright.

"What did you tell them about the family, Smiley?"

My mouth is so dry I have to pull my lips apart to speak. "Nothing, Starkey. I didn't tell them anything about us." It's the truth, but my eyes fill up and my tight throat won't allow me to say more. My legs tingle under me, and I shift my butt. That's when I realize I've peed my pants.

The bearded man, Seattle, stands up. "It's a little late, Starkey. Your family looks done in." He holds up a bottle. "And you and I need to catch up on things over a nightcap."

The circle rustles, adjusts itself, looks at its father. Starkey shrugs. "We aren't in a hurry to teach this particular lesson. Tomorrow morning." He slips the knife into its holder, then the holder into his pocket, stands and comes toward me. When he smells the pee, he makes a face, says, "God, she's a mess," and tells Jasper to tie me up, then cover me with Leaky's damp bag. He and Seattle move off toward the tent Starkey sleeps in.

"I still have to go," I say to the boy, and he leads me out of the circle and to a bush hanging over the latrine ditch. He hangs onto my hair as I pull down my underpants and squat. "You really in deep shit, girl," he says as he ties my hands behind me. I can't tell if he's cracking a joke or scared. I decide scared when I feel his fingers shaking on my arm. He leads me back to the fire, wraps another rope around my ankles. I'm not crying anymore, but Leaky is, his arm over his eyes, his mouth curved into a tight-lipped pucker like he's in pain. Someone lays a blanket over him, and I whisper, "Goodnight, Leaky."

Then I try working the ropes holding me, and I understand that I will not escape this time. The family is quiet; only the sputtering fire and an occasional laugh from the tent break into the stillness. Then in the starlit silence, I hear the rustling of leaves and know someone else can't sleep either, may even be using my bush.

CHAPTER THIRTY-SIX

ELLIE

SEPTEMBER 2009

She's been gone almost three days, and I've had plenty of time to think. My son is haunting me, but so is Sarah. I know what the graffiti, the orange smiley face, is saying. She's in danger, or was, before she left. The family in the woods is looking for her, and I'm guessing they don't know about her staying in this building. If they did, they would have waited for her right on the front steps. But they do know that she has been around the park. Sarah should not come back here. I need to warn her, but I don't know where she is. Maybe that's good—the fewer who know, the better. Nothing I can do.

About Danny, either. He's a grown-up man now, still simmering with hatred for his mother, I suppose. He hasn't tried to contact me since that time I told him I wouldn't send him money. Nine years.

I wonder if I would even recognize him. Maybe his eyes. I'm different, too. Clean and sober doesn't mean you look better. In fact, I look a lot older without the hair dye, despite my nightly rubbing in of Pond's. I'd probably look younger if I thought clothes were important, and maybe lipstick. And if I ever had a decent night's sleep.

Then tonight, sleepless, I have a revelation about Sarah and Danny. I understand that I might have it all wrong, what is happening. Sarah kept hinting she'd seen Danny somewhere when she looked at his picture. But he hasn't been in this town for years, since she was a little kid. Or has he? Since he left, something in me has been waiting for him to come back and make his threat good, to pay me back for the life I handed him.

Maybe he *is* back. Maybe Sarah has seen him on the street somewhere. Maybe . . . and then, somewhere in the craziness of early morning half-dreams, it hits me, and I wake all the way up, panting, upright. I know why she recognized Danny. Starkey. Same age, tall, tells a god-awful story about a bad childhood. Not Danny's childhood, bad as it was, but one even worse, to explain his behavior. The evil grandfather could have been an evil mother, the sex stuff invented to get kids to talk about their own terrible lives, the frightening disguise, the bandanna and the whiskers, a hook to pull his recruits into his circle and keep them there.

"I'll pay you back for this goddamn life," my son said. And now this is payback time. He's killing people with his father's ivory-handled hunting knife and leaving the bodies within steps of me. He's threatening Sarah, maybe because she's run away and has chosen me over him. He's known all along where she was. Playing with us. He is heading in my direction, murder by murder. And he's furious because now Sarah has escaped him. That leaves me.

Sleep-deprived panic city, I tell myself, but I don't go back to sleep. I sit up in the dark until morning, and now I'm drinking lukewarm instant and thinking those same heart-stopping thoughts in the broad daylight. They still make sense. They explain it all. My son is back.

I write out a note to the super, breaking my lease. I am leaving in four days, I say, when the rent is due. Sorry for the short notice. Something came up. After I shove the note under his door, I go out and get one of those free newspapers that list apartments for rent. And I go to the bank and take out my savings, enough for first and last month's rent. Then

I pick up a couple of boxes and a jar of coffee from the 7-Eleven, and I come home.

A couple of boxes aren't enough, not even for the kitchen stuff. I put the water on for coffee, wonder if anyone in the building has extra boxes. Probably, the way some of them move around. Then I hear a sound, like a baby crying at my door. *What now?*

I open the door. It is not a baby. It is Sarah, covered in blood, reaching out for me.

Welts and bruises surge on what I can see of her body. One eye is purple, and when I get her clothes off, I see where the blood is coming from. Someone has carved a smiley face on her arm, has crossed it out. The last slash is deep enough to show muscle and bone beneath it.

Sarah faints as I clean and bandage her. At times, I can't see what I'm doing and have to stop and wipe away the blood. And the tears running down my face. I slow the flow of blood from between her legs with a towel, wrap her in the Japanese robe and get her to the bed. As I cover her with my quilt, she stirs.

"Thank you, Ellie," she says, and then she closes her eyes again. I put my cheek to hers, feel her breath on my ear, her warm skin on mine. She's alive.

Then I hear it. The smoke alarm. The kettle has burned dry on the stove. I hurry to the kitchen, hoping it hasn't melted onto the burner, like it did once before, and as I turn off the heat, I hear a knock at the door. Someone nearby thinks I'm burning down the building. I go to explain, and it is the super, on a mission. I have a phone call, he tells me, and could I turn off the alarm if the crisis is over? I hand him the broom and tell him to do it himself while I go to the phone, put the receiver to my ear.

"Careful," a man breathes. "You're in troub. . .le." I stand there listening to silence and realizing that the voice I've just heard is my son's, ten years older.

I run back to my apartment, lock the door, shove the leather chair against it, and go into the bedroom.

I sit next to Sarah all day. Her forehead doesn't feel hot, and the next time she wakes up she can talk a little. She tells me how she went back to the family to warn the kids that the police were going to search the forest. But Starkey caught her, kept her tied up, told the family that because she was disloyal, she would be an example to them.

The next day he made everyone hit her with their fists and call her names, even Leaky, who couldn't stop crying. Only Owl, the retarded girl, and a couple of new kids hit hard, so Starkey made the rest of them use the bat. Sarah passed out, and when she woke up, Lila was washing her off, taking off her wet clothes and putting a pair of her own jeans on her.

" 'Shush,' Lila whispered. Starkey's in his tent.' Lila's nice," Sarah adds, her eyelids at half-mast.

"Sleep," I tell her. "There's plenty of time to talk about this." She closes her eyes.   What I have plenty of time to do is think. I am responsible for her pain, for the blood seeping through the gauze I've wrapped around her still arm. For the red towel under her. I jump when I hear noises in the hall. They move on. I keep thinking.

I am the one who said to leave things be, don't get involved, the one who believed that a person should take care of herself. But I don't know what to do about this girl, this Sarah, about the phone call from my son. So I sit by the bed, watch the bruised eye become more purple, the color move down her cheek like a flood of hurt. When she wakes up again, midnight, she is hungry, and I find a can of soup in the boxes I've tried to pack. I feed her and she goes on with her story, as if its telling will make the horror go away.

That afternoon, she says, Starkey took off his belt and beat it against Lila's back. He'd recognized the clean jeans she'd given Sarah. Then he sent the family out and told them to bring back a feast. They'd have a party that evening.

The celebration began with Dumpster pizza and stolen bottled tea. "Dessert," Sarah said, pushing back against her pillow at the last spoonful of soup, "was me."

"Bebop brought out his white plastic bucket and when Starkey raised the bat, he began a slow rattle, his drumsticks, smooth branches moving like tiny jackhammers, scaring me. They'd untied my arms, made me lie down." Sarah swallows and keeps going, her voice so soft I have to lean in close. "Kids' feet held down each of my hands. Starkey took out his knife and pressed it into my arm. He cut across the freesia, Ellie." She looks at her arm, wrapped, still bleeding a little. "Then I blacked out again."

I give her a glass of water, and in a few minutes she continues, her story so terrible I breathe in gulps, like someone is choking me.

When she came to, the new guy was pulling Starkey away from her, yelling at him, and the kids were huddled on the far side of the fire, cringing away from the tangle of bodies crashing around them, spewing clouds of dust and fir needles into the air. Only Mouse stood watching the two men go at it, the homemade drumstick in his hand, its wet point shining in the red flames of the fire.

"Then Jimmy leaned over me, yanked me up, told me to run fast, and he wrapped his sweatshirt around my arm. And I ran, heading down in my bare feet, through the blackberries, around Doug firs, crashing through the bushes, flying, maybe, finally lying down under a roof of ferns, falling into some kind of sleep. When I opened my eyes, blue sky leaked between the fronds, and below me was the water tower."

Sarah's feet twitch under the blankets. I'll let her look at them, coated with Mercurochrome and wrapped in strips of torn-up sheet, some other time. I nod to encourage her to keep talking.

"I crawled, hanging on to rocks and trees with my one arm, zigzagging down the hill, resting when I found a flat spot, until I came to the official trail, the signs pointing to the forest's trailhead, the park, and the street to your house. I don't remember very much of this last part."

Sarah sighs, grimaces. "I just knew you'd be here." Then she goes back to sleep.

I cannot move. Sarah's hell has become mine. We'll each have to deal with it. For once, this *is* my business. The beaten girl in front of me has taught me that even an old lady needs to face life, fight for something, for someone. Even if it means facing her son one more time. This time, neither of us will run away.

By the time she wakes up again, I have a plan.

CHAPTER THIRTY-SEVEN

SARAH

SEPTEMBER 2009

I don't tell her all of it, of course. I can't find the words to tell her, not when her face is so white, her eyes wide with disbelief and something else. Pain. My pain, shooting in waves from my arm to my chest and into her. And the other pain, flowing from between my legs. Ellie thinks I'm miscarrying. She's tucked a towel under me, tells me it's going to be okay, I'll maybe even be glad someday, even if I did care for Peter. Someday when I'm ready, someday when I . . . I love her for saying these words, like a mother might, for not seeing how this red river just keeps coming, no lumps of tiny baby, just blood.

She's spooning soup into me again. I like the spoon coming at me in a steady rhythm, the way my mouth opens to receive it, the way she says, "Good girl."

Ellie gives me a pill, leftover, she says, from when she had a bad cut a long time ago, but it's probably still good enough to keep infection away. Now I need to sleep, she says. I feel her checking my arm, looking at the torn petals, the butterfly bandages and gauze she's stretched over the blossoms. Her hand slips under the quilt, changes the towel, and I hear her take a breath, walk to the sink, run the water over the cloth, say, "Oh, oh."

I wake up because the bed is dipping with the weight of her sitting next to me. "I need to ask you some questions," she says. "When I'm finished, you will go to the ER to make sure you are doing okay." She has a pencil and a pad in her hand; she looks serious, like what I answer will be important to whatever she is going to do. I'm not sure I will tell her anything else. I can still feel Leaky's nervous foot, see Jimmy's fear-shot eyes as he wrapped his sweatshirt around me. I don't want to go through it again, not even in my mind.

"What?" I ask. I can't't look at her.

"No need to get upset. I just need to know where that camp is, what part of the forest. No, don't do that. Look at me. I'm not going to call the police. I want to help your friends, Leaky and Jimmy and Lila, like they helped you. I just need to know how to find the camp."

She's too old to think like this. What can she possibly do? "No way will you find it. I got lost when I went up by myself this time. It's really hard to tell you where to go. The trails run all over, with signs on the real ones, nothing on the little paths where most people don't go. It's impossible."

"Please, Sarah. I have another reason for finding the camp. It has nothing to do with you, all to do with me. I can't tell you, but you have to trust me. I need to get up there, right away."

When she sees that I'm not talking, she turns my head toward her, forces me to meet her eyes. "I got a phone call from someone up there, I don't know who. The voice threatened me, us, maybe, said I was in trouble, like I should watch out. I've got to understand why. An old lady. I mind my own business. I may not have friends, but I don't have enemies, either. Until now."

She's thinking about Rick, maybe. And about Peter. No enemies, but dead anyway.

"And something you don't know. A fourteen–year-old boy was found dead on the play equipment a few days ago. Why would someone kill a kid like that?"

He tried to phone home, that's why. Starkey laughed when he talked about Sampson. I think of

Leaky and Jimmy and the frightened looks on their faces. I think of Jimmy giving me his sweatshirt, maybe getting caught after I got away. But this old woman can't do what she says she's going to do— walk into camp, save the kids. Not all by herself.

"No," I say. I can't bear the thought of losing Ellie, too. I roll my body toward the wall, even though I can feel blood moving out of me with the turning.

Her hand touches my back. "Sarah," she whispers, "I am the cause of those dead people. I am responsible for creating the monster who is forcing the family to be his killers. I am the mother who didn't love her son enough to stick with him during his bad times. I am a selfish old woman who minded her own business."

I can hear her choking sobs, and I turn back to her. Her head is on the bed, her fingers pressing into the quilt.

"I don't understand."

"Starkey is my son, Danny." Her muffled, anguished words frighten me, make me move my throbbing arm to touch her hair. "He called to tell me I was in some sort of trouble, a jab to torture me, to tell me that he has returned to pay me back like he promised."

We are silent for a while. Then she raises her head and says, calm and straight—like she's moved on to the next part of a plan, her tears the fuel to get her on her way— "When you come into the forest from the downtown, how do you go? It must be different than coming up from the park, especially with the heavy stuff you might be carrying."

She is right. There is a longer way to the top of the forest, a road cut into the hillside on its far edge. Lila said that the road was for fire trucks, and we laughed because the little creek we lived by wouldn't put out anything larger than a campfire. "They bring the water up, stupid," she said, like she knew. "I saw it once on TV. In California."

If Ellie could find the road, go to the top, and then come down, she might be able to get to the camp. But then what? "That's nuts, Ellie." I'm feeling woozy and sick to my stomach. "I might throw up."

"Not yet," she says. "What did you just think of?" She's so close I breathe in her coffee breath, the paper and pencil forgotten.

I tell her. "A road, from the other end of downtown. I only did it once. You have to go up the busy highway that cuts through the hills. We walked on a bike path," I remember. "It's longer but easier than climbing up the hills in the trees. We turned in where a sign says something about 'the county forest ends here.' A road goes along a fence, with other paths branching off from it. I don't know which one we took. We just dropped down until we saw the tent and smelled the fire. We had to hang on to roots and limbs to get down."

Ellie nods, stands up.

"You're too old, Ellie."

She shakes her head. "Not this time."

Now I'm really scared, for Leaky and Jimmy, for the other kids, too, but especially for her. "Wait a few days, until I feel better. I can help." Even as I say the words, I know I can't. I'm out of help. *I* need help, in fact, and the knock at the door lets me know that Ellie knows that too. She lifts me up from the pillow and wraps the quilt around me, and the super leads two men and a gurney through the doorway.

"She's been attacked," Ellie says. "You'll need to get the police involved. But first she needs to stop bleeding, get stitched up."

"Are you family?" the attendant asks. He has papers in his hand, pointing them at Ellie.

"Yes, I'm her grandmother. I'll sign whatever I need to sign when I meet her at the hospital. She doesn't have insurance."

Fifteen minutes later, I am lying on a bed in the ER, a nurse unwrapping my bandages, removing Ellie's towel, saying nothing but tightening her lips as she throws it into the basket. I let myself be handled. Something in the tube they've stuck into my arm removes me from them, from the lights above me, from the ache in my arm, the shooting pains in my stomach.

When I wake up, I am in a room that looks out to a wooded hill. A TV is sending ocean scenes toward me; soft music makes me wonder if I'm in some kind of heaven. Then I see her. A woman in a dark blue uniform. She smiles.

"Welcome back," she says.

CHAPTER THIRTY-EIGHT

ELLIE

SEPTEMBER 2009

I am relieved when the ambulance rolls away. Sarah is safe. Now it's time for me to get moving. I need a way to get up the highway to the top. I'm thinking it will be a couple of miles uphill before I find the fire road. An exhausted old woman sitting along the side of a busy road will bring too much attention, the cops, maybe, with calls on cell phones from cars whizzing by. I need to disappear, and I need something to help me make my way up there, like a walker or a scooter or something I can hang on to.

Then I remember Rick's cart under the stairs, still full of cans. I go to my closet and take out an old winter overcoat I got at Goodwill years ago, a rain hat, the kind old ladies wear with flaps that cover ears, tie under the chin, a scarf I found on the side-walk, my oldest sneakers. I put them on, and I am invisible. An old homeless woman leaning against a slow-going cart full of bottles and cans doesn't exist for most everyone she passes. Maybe even for herself.

I open the silverware drawer and take out my butcher knife, slip it into my deep pocket. I've had this knife forever. An Italian chef in a red apron is carved into on its wooden handle—not a hunting knife, of course, but it has a blade narrowed to a point over the years on the gray stone lying next to it. It is sharp enough to cut through chicken bones.

How fitting it will be to meet my son with such a weapon, a family heirloom of sorts. I dig through the sink cabinet for the pepper spray, and the can goes into another pocket. I can't think of anything else to bring along. My guilt is the heaviest weapon I carry.

No one is in the entry when I push out with Rick's cart. I cross the park, look at the children playing on the slide where the boy's body was found, notice that fresh bark dust has been laid there. I'm glad a cool breeze is loosening the last reluctant leaves from the maples, sending yellow good-byes into the air. I'll be very warm once I walk through downtown, head up the highway. Already my overcoat is building up steam, but I don't take it off.

The streets are bright with orange and red shop windows. Halloween is coming in a few weeks, then Thanksgiving. Some women I pass are already wearing scarves and leather boots, men in warm jackets or overcoats that look heavy, like the one on my back. I blend in, using the handicap sidewalk ramps and the benches scattered every few blocks to rest. I notice that when I sit down, the person sitting on the other end of the bench scoots away or gets up, without looking at me. No one will remember me; no one wants to talk to me, wants to know where I'm going, what I'm doing.

The intersection where the highway meets the main street confuses me. The sidewalks end. Then a bike swirls by and I see that it is moving alongside the traffic in the narrow lane marked for bicycles. And carts, I'm assuming. I begin the push uphill.

No benches line up on this busy road, and as I put one foot in front of the other, I find myself leaning hard on the cart, my body doing the pushing now, my back bent and beginning to ache. Bushes spread onto the asphalt on the right side of the road, and when I see a break in them, I shove the cart into it and lower myself down to the ground next to it. I can't quit now, but I'm not sure I can go on, either. I must be nuts.

A city bus slows down in front of me, stops at the sign I've not noticed until now, its driver gesturing at me. *Get in*, he mouths. I half get up, grab at the cart, know I have a way out of all this, a dollar in my pocket to get me over the hill and beyond. My bending body brings a sharp stab in my thigh. The point of the knife is reminding me I have a job to do, a girl to save, a son's craziness to end, a sin to erase. *No, sorry*, I mouth back, waving my hand; the bus rumbles off, leaving me in a cloud of fumes. I straighten up, say now or never to my legs, and begin up the bike path again. I *am* nuts, I decide, but it's all right. What else is there?

An hour later, I see the sign: COUNTY FOREST BOUNDARY. A wire fence cuts into the trees; a path, wide enough for my cart, runs along it. Feet have beaten down the weeds, left ridges I have to watch out for. They unsettle both me and the cart. A drift of plastic bottles and bags lines the fence and the underbrush. Somewhere in my head I make a note to come up here sometime and clean this mess up. Garbage Grandma, my next occupation, if I have a chance to have one. *One thing at a time*, I tell myself.

"We saw the smoke and the tent and headed down," Sarah said. Narrow paths lead down from the one I am on, and I follow one for a couple of yards, but I can see no sign of a camp. I am glad to get back to the cart, which I am beginning to hang on to as if it is a part of me. I've taken off the coat, tossed it over the bags of cans and bottles and tucked in its edges to help keep it all inside the basket as I bump over tree roots and animal holes. The holes are small, squirrel size, and I don't expect a growling, furry head to pop out at me. Then I think of snakes. I keep moving, tugging, pushing, aiming the cart north. I know it's north because my back, even without the coat, is wet, sweat angling down my backside, making me pause and scratch. Then the sun moves west, and I pull my cap down over my left cheek to keep it from getting burned.

I am definitely certifiable, worrying about being burned by sinking fall sun when I am on a suicide mission and at the moment am very close to waving a white flag and admitting defeat. I sit down and try to pull myself together.

Then I see it, through the Oregon grape in front of me: a brown hump of a tent a long way off, a canvas chair in front of it. If I hadn't been trying to get comfortable, squatting and twisting on a sharp rock, I would have missed it. I stay down, trying to think what to do next. I find myself remembering why I knew that the bush in front of me is Oregon grape.

Danny, when he was still my Danny, went off to Outdoor School, and his present to me on his return after four days in the woods was a prickly branch of something he called Oregon grape. It was special, he said. You could make jam from its berries. We put it in a glass of water and hoped it would grow roots. It didn't. Maybe one of the last things we tried to do together.

Not helpful, I tell myself. This one looks dead, too. I look beyond the bush in front of me. This is as far as Rick's cart can go.

The homeless costume was to make me invisible as I moved through downtown and up the busy road. The cart was my walker. The cans in the cart . . . That's it. I am a homeless old woman with a bag of cans I will offer in exchange for a place to sleep for a night, for whatever food I can scrounge from the campers. I rub a little more dirt on my face, pull down my hat, and put my coat back on, pry the black plastic bag filled with cans out of the cart and begin down the path. I can say I've lost the wool blanket they gave me at the shelter somewhere. The only things of value are a few bottles in the cart and my bag of cans, which at the moment is threatening to break open as branches poke into it, to pull me sideways into what something, maybe another Danny memory, tells me is poison oak.

I balance the bag on my shoulder, holding it with one hand. The other hand reaches out for roots and rocks. I slip, land on my seat a few times. My knee feels like it's bleeding, but I can't stop the going down.

I have no idea what will happen next, except maybe it includes a little food. I can smell beans warming up.

CHAPTER THIRTY-NINE

SARAH

SEPTEMBER 2009

She's young, the policewoman. Her hair is pulled back against her neck; her eyes look at me through blue-tinted lashes. When she speaks, her teeth, white and straight, flash at me. "Welcome back," she says.

I throw up. I'm getting good at it.

"It's the meds," she says. "They do that sometimes."

A nurse, or whatever she is in her flowered smock, changes the sheet, tucks me in again. I realize I don't hurt and also that I don't know what day it is, where I am. The policewoman introduces herself. "Angie," she says, and asks me my name. "I'm not sure," I answer.

"Think."

"Smiley, I guess." Then it all starts to flood back into my unwilling mind. "I've got to go up into the camp," I say, because I remember now what Ellie is trying to do, know what will happen to her. "They'll kill her."

Then, not caring how I sound, I let sentences slither in and out of my mouth, words collide into nonsense. I care only that someone is listening, taking notes, calling on her cell phone.

"She's talking," she says.

"Ellie's up there, at the camp." I go off somewhere black for a while. When I wake up, Sergeant Trommald is leaning over me. "What camp?"

"The family's camp. Starkey and a bunch of kids."

"Where?"

I can't answer. How can I tell him when all he knows is the city park, the boundary trail at its edge, the official forest trails? "Off the real trails, the ones with the signs," I say. "Start there, by the play equipment. That's the fastest way."

"Then what?"

"Find the little paths, animal trails." Then I see it. My pack under a tree just before the path leading up, up to the smell of the latrine, the campfire. "First, look for my duffel," I say. "Keep going up until you see the old water tank. Then look for smoke." I disappear back into the blackness.

Angie the cop is still there when I wake up. I ache all over, and I realize something is still pressing between my legs. My arm is bandaged, secured at my waist with some sort of belt. My feet hurt. My mouth is dry. "Water," I say.

"Sure." She holds the cup, waits for me to ask.

I do. "What?"

She tells me that my arm is stitched together and it seems okay. No infection yet. The tattoo might even make it with just a little crunch in the stem. She smiles. "Your feet are a mess, but not a bad mess." She gets serious. "Your vagina also has been repaired with stitches. The doctors think they have saved your uterus, but you lost a lot of blood." She pauses. "Do you remember what happened to you?"

I remember being held down. I remember watching the knife cut into my arm. I don't want to remember anything else. All I can say is, "Was I pregnant?"

"If you were, not anymore." Angie has taken my hand, is rubbing a knuckle, looking bluely at me. "But you are going to be okay. And," she adds, as if she knows it's my next question, "we're out looking for your friend."

She sits back down in the chair under the TV screen, and I watch the beautiful forest scenes pass by. Somewhere among those scenes I see a knife peeling bark from a fallen branch I've brought back for the fire. I see the branch, now smooth, a drumstick, its knobs and pointed end held over me. I see Starkey grinning through gritted teeth, his hand guiding Mouse's hand, whose fingers curl around the stick as it comes toward me.

CHAPTER FORTY

JEFF

SEPTEMBER 2009

When the old woman turns toward him, Starkey is flummoxed. What in hell is he going to do with a senile old bitch?

He has just planned the most important ritual of this or any family's experience, the condemnation of the sin of false friendship. He has his words prepared, the weapons sharp, the punishment so very appropriate for this ultimate disloyalty that his adrenaline surges in anticipation. With this old woman in the camp, the ceremony, flowing with ancient symbolism, will be tainted with her non-symbolic death as an intruder.

Something about her. He surveys her dirty face, grimy coat, her slump of a body.

Fuck! The crone in the plaid coat is Danny's mother. Serendipity or dumb luck? Whatever, the stars have aligned for this evening's events, a sign that this event is ordained. Not only the traitorous son, but also the mother who is the cause of the shambles Starkey's life is edging toward. Both will find themselves on the altar this evening. Both will pay for their deceit. And there will be no more Smiley disasters. His family will flourish once again.

Starkey smiles, points the old woman toward the latrine.

Two nights ago, Smiley's punishment ritual proceeded as he had planned. She lay on a tarp, the family standing watch a few feet away. Her whimpers warmed him, but her bleeding arm was only the beginning. Starkey had instructed Mouse about his responsibility in this ceremony, but he saw that Mouse's arm hung limp at his side, the stick held loosely, about to drop, his wide, glazed eyes proof of this son's underlying cowardice.

Angry, Starkey reached out, wrapped his fingers around the boy's fist. In one long movement he guided the drumstick between the girl's open legs, into the waiting vagina, plunged it against soft tissue as Mouse's screams joined the girl's.

At that moment, Starkey felt his knees crumple and he fell to the ground. A hand pressed his face into the dirt. He kicked, heaved himself onto his back, shoved at the chest above him. Then he heard the *thunk* of a head striking one of the rocks circling the fire. He pulled himself upright, saw Danny lying next to him, his eyes closed. His attacker remained stunned long enough to allow Starkey to stand up, grab the bat, and beat his friend into unconsciousness.

Then, his breath rasping in ragged gasps, Starkey made his way his chair, sat down, looked out over the fire. His family huddled under a mound of blackberry bushes. The girl was nowhere.

He ordered his children to come to him, and they crept out of the shadows and stood in front of the fire. At his command, they carried Seattle into the tent, then rolled up in their bags at the edge of the camp and let the coals cool. If they spoke, it was with eyes blank with fear, just as their father wished.

Last night, Starkey, lying beside an unconscious Danny, recalled his hard-on as his hand gripped Mouse's fist, and he worked a little to bring it back, then gave up. He had made a bad mistake. Again. He'd ignored the recent furtive glances, the mumbled words as the kids went off to do their chores, the stiff mouths as they frowned at his rhetorical questions during his lessons. He had to come up with a way to bring his family back from the ashes before he lost them.

Ritual had been effective when the stakes were lower, when disloyalty could be dealt with by a few strokes of a bat. "Cudgeling," they had called it. Heart-revving drumbeats built to a climax, the sacred knife gleamed in the light of the fire, the bat hit flesh.

Wide-awake on his cot, Starkey reached into his rucksack, felt for a piece of paper, unreadable in the dark tent. Sometimes when he lost sight of the path he had chosen, began to doubt the reality of his vision, he took out this talisman, touched the heart she had drawn years before. The note was warmed by his mother, the beautiful red-lipped woman who had held him on her lap and offered him the only love he'd ever known. Life as it unfolded had offered only the smothering weight of unlove and abandonment. As always, holding his mother's words in his hand, he could feel her presence, knew she was watching, believed in him.

He waited a moment and knew what to do.

He sat up. The same year he'd read the pirate book that guided his new persona, he had also checked out a book from the school library about the Aztecs. He had been fascinated by the picture of the pyramid, the stone altar at its peak, the drain catching the blood, the beating heart held up to the sun by the bronzed arms of a fierce warrior. Human blood was the gods' proper nourishment; human sacrifice kept the gods from destroying the universe. He had torn the picture out of the book and tacked it to his wall.

The possibility of restoring order to his life, to protecting his universe, through a mystical sacrifice pleased him. He'd have to keep Danny alive, of course.

He folded the paper, felt the easing of an edge that meant it had torn a little more, and slipped it back into the pocket of his pack. And, just as carefully, he covered the still body lying beside him with his jacket.

Now, a day later, with Mrs. Miller in the camp, the plan takes on a whole new dimension.

He invites her to join them at dinner. She accepts a plate and settles on a rock near the fire. He enjoys watching her fidget with her food, whisper to Leaky, who doesn't answer her, glance around the camp, look for escape.

A hand of fate brought her here. Even if Danny had actually gotten in contact with her with his cell phone, no way could she have made her way up into the forest without divine guidance. This ceremony was predestined.

Then he notices her shoes, red sneakers, familiar because Smiley wore similar ones, had made her escape leaving behind a pair just like them. Apparently this old woman has fucked him over not just once, with one kid, but twice, with another, all three of them traitors. Mrs. Miller deserves to be punished even more than Danny and Smiley. She is responsible for everything.

The ritual will be a living hell for her. Her hands will hold her son's beating heart to the sun. His blood, draining into the earth, will appease the gods and offer retribution for her evil acts. Starkey retreats to his tent to prepare.

After the family has cleaned up the debris of the meal, Starkey opens the tent flaps and emerges, his bandanna now a band tied around his forehead. One white feather rises above his head. A black bird, its one nippled eye glaring, spreads its wings across his bare chest. He bathes in the stunned silence of the campfire as he leans against the canvas back of his throne. Then he points at the white plastic bucket next to his chair. Bebop kneels at his drum, looks up at the chieftain, and picks up the drumsticks. As the drumbeats reach an ear-shattering crescendo, Starkey waves a hand, its palm stained black from the charcoaled wood that created the raven. Bebop stops, slips back into the circle, wipes his forehead on his sleeve.

Starkey leans forward, begins to speak. The words flow from his throat as if they have been waiting forever for this moment. At first he talks of spring, redemption, nature's and the gods' willingness to allow their lives to continue unabated. Then he lowers his voice to a soft growl. "We must be willing to pay the price for this blessing. Tonight." The tension in his throat and the wary eyes watching him inform Starkey that the time has come.

He rises and enters his tent. In the dim light making its way through a half-opened flap, he sees the hump that is his once-friend, silent but alive still. Starkey's hands tremble, and he understands that this is the most momentous event of his life. He breathes, calms himself, bends to scatter a handful of fragrant fir needles over the still body. Then he grasps it by its loose legs and drags it out of the tent toward the fire, leaving a bloody path to the wooden plank where the food once was. He places Danny on this altar, arranges fir boughs around him.

He walks back to his chair. "You know this man as Seattle. I know him as Traitor." He glances around the circle of his silent children to make sure the cudgel and the sacred knife are in their places, that a chest is still rising in shallow breaths, that an evil mother's eyes are brimming with tears.

GRAFFITI GRANDMA

CHAP

I hear a moan,
to leak from the
I am mov
another w
"Who a

I stumble into the camp, the black plastic bag falling off my shoulders and onto the feet of a teenager, who stares at me and then bends to help me pick up the spilled cans. Her flat features and slow-lidded eyes tell me she is a little dull, but her smile lets me know I don't have to be worried. I look around. The two of us are alone.

"Hello?" I say. She continues to smile. No help here. The tent is set up a few yards from the ring of stones and blankets that surround the fire pit. To one side of the pit, a couple of pans pile up, and a pot hangs over the fire that must be the source of the beans' aroma. The girl is in charge of the cooking. Others are away, doing chores, maybe, collecting whatever else the meal will hold.

a word. "Water." The sound seems
tent.

ng in that direction when I am hit by
rd, this one frightening. "Stop." Then,
e you, and why are you here?"

urn. The man has skinny devil eyes. A slit of a
uth slices through a neat beard. His deep voice
would curdle cream. A kerchief, knotted at the back
of his head, covers his hair. A gold ring dangles from
one ear.

"Hello?" I try again. I go into an old-woman
hunch, try to look more even pathetic than I feel. "I
saw your camp, thought I could exchange my cans
for a little food. I haven't eaten in a while, and," I try
to chuckle, "there aren't any return machines here
in the woods." I point at the cans, the girl clutching
the neck of the bag. She looks from the man to me.

He seems to be smiling, the edges of his mustache moving upward, his eyes even more narrow.
"Of course. Welcome," he says, and he points to
bushes beyond the ring. "We have a latrine if you
need it. Feel free, and then come back and enjoy the
fire. And Owl, take the cans to the recycling area.
We'll turn them in tomorrow."

My nose is now aware of the latrine, and I am
heading toward it when he adds, "Glad you're here.

We've never done an old woman before." I don't know what he means. A threat? Can he possibly know why I'm here? And where is Danny?

When I get back to the fire, Owl is bending into the tent, a cup of water dripping in front of her. A moment later I hear a thin thank-you. Owl smiles as she backs out, wiping her hands on her jacket.

The pirate pushes aside the tent flap and calls to me over his shoulder as he crawls through the opening, "Sit down and make yourself comfortable. The rest of the family will be back any minute." I hear a bottle clink against a glass once he's inside.

Then kids start pouring in from all directions. One of them, a black boy, says he found a cart up above the camp with a few bottles in it. "Mine," I say, and "yours if you want them. I'm," and I hesitate, "Grandma. Who are you?" When I hold out my hand, he wraps his fat fingers around it.

"Bebop, and this here is Jasper." The other boy, his curly hair gasoline-red, nods and looks into the pot on the fire. "That all?" he says.

"Be glad of it, dildo." A gangly girl in camouflage and a khaki knit cap steps into the warmth of the fire. "You had it too good lately. I almost starved last week until Lila found me, brought me here." She high-fives a girl who looks like a bedraggled Asian princess, her lacy edges brown with dirt. The net petticoat she's wearing on the outside of her jeans hangs in lazy droops at her ankles.

So this is Lila, tough, nice Lila. Not so tough. Frightened, if her solemn eyes aren't lying.

The camouflaged girl looks at me. "How's it hanging?" It's been a long time since I heard that greeting.

"Loosey goosey," I answer. I hope I sound like a senile old woman.

"Just Goose," she says. "How'd you guess?" Goose settles herself next to me, and I see that her camouflage is not army issue. Big green and gray birds fly across her chest and up her arms.

"You must be a hunter."

"My dad is, or used to be a few years ago."

I don't ask for the details. None of my business.

I'm noticing that for teenagers, they're pretty quiet. They keep looking at the tent, at each other, as they spread out the food they've brought on the plywood board in front of the fire. Then they sit down in the rock circle, wait.

"Where's Mouse?" someone asks.

"Mouse got picked up hustling in Chinatown. He won't be back for a day or so." Lila pokes at the ground with a twig, not looking up.

"I bet," Jasper says. "Wait till Starkey hears about that."

A low hum of "uh huhs" ends abruptly.

"I've heard about it."

I turn. If this skanky-eyed, bandannaed fool is Starkey, then Starkey is not my son. I have miscalculated. A wave of relief almost drowns me. My next thought is *Why am I here?* Then, more to the point, *So what's the plan?* I don't have one now that I don't have a son to kill.

"We'll deal with Mouse's bad decision another time. Eat. We have a ceremony planned for tonight, as you well know. And we have an unexpected guest." He taps my shoulder, and I try to, but can't, smile at the eyes looking at me. They aren't smiling, either.

Owl ladles out beans onto our paper plates, and we line up and choose bits of other food from the board. I take a roll, pick off the mold, sit back down and pretend I'm eating. A boy, narrow and spindly-looking in skintight jeans, dark hair falling onto his forehead, black eyes taking me in, sits down on Goose's rock. His voice is soft, a whisper. "I'm Leaky," he says. His hands tremble as he shoves a pile of beans toward his mouth.

I whisper back, "You helped Sarah." Then I notice the bruise under the bangs, the ear bloody and bandaged. "He found out?"

"We all got punished. That's why Mouse isn't here. Ellie, you're in trouble." This is the second time I've been warned with these words. Must be true. The boy glances over my shoulder, shuts up.

Starkey knows who I am. Sarah must have said something to him about me. About an old lady who took her in for a while, like a grandma. How did he recognize me? Then I know. My red shoes, just like the ones she wore when she came back to this camp, huddle under the bulk of me perched on the rock.

Who else did she tell about me? Maybe the kid who is taking my plate and tossing it with his into the fire. Short and a little pudgy, his belly showing below his T-shirt. Oily strands of long blond hair separate to reveal red stripes on his neck, dots of blood on his shoulders. He lays a scrap of blanket on the ground, sits at my feet. Jimmy.

The fire flares with the plates and scraps of food. Everyone is silent. Then Starkey emerges from his tent, bending so that the feather sticking up from the band tied around his head misses the flaps. He's changed from a pirate to some kind of painted Indian. His hands are black like the black he's smeared on his body and on his cheekbones. His transformation has frightened the kids into gasps, and me into a hysterical giggle. *What next?* I ask myself, and I don't think I want to know.

He settles into his chair, says, "Begin, Bebop," and the beat of a stick on a plastic bucket fills the air, joining the smoke and fear floating around us.

Bebop's rhythm races into a thunderclap, then stops. Starkey lifts his chin, and slowly he looks us over. Then he holds a bat upright. "Tonight we deal with the disloyalty of a broken friendship, the worst kind of betrayal. A friend I considered a true companion on the road of life, from my childhood on, turned on me, allowed our sister to run away yet another time, and because of his disloyalty, all of you have been punished." Starkey takes a cell phone from his pocket, places it on the rock, brings the bat down on it. "Who knows the damage this betrayal has done?"

He pauses. "However, tonight we also must deal with another kind of disloyalty. A good father teaches his children that the failure to act can be as evil as committing a sin." He passes an uplifted palm over a circle of unblinking eyes. "Who of you stood up to defend me when I was attacked? No one. You all cowered, watched, allowed our fugitive sister to escape. And who tried to bring her back?"

I feel an arm rise beside me. "Me. I followed her," Leaky says.

"Faggot effort," Starkey spits out.

"I got lost."

"Enough. We have work to do." Starkey gets up, disappears into the tent. He comes out dragging a slump of a naked man blue with bruises, patched with dried blood. He lays the body down on the board that held our dinner. "You know him as Seattle. I know him as Traitor."

And I know him as my son. I must have made a sound, because Jimmy tightens his hand on my knee. *Be quiet*, his touch urges.

"Tonight we go beyond punishing disloyalty. We go to the core of our very existence. Lila, bring the instruments to me." Lila scuttles to the throne, picks up the bat and something else. He points to the rock at the end of the board. "There."

She leans the bat against the rock and places a leather-sheathed knife in one of its crevices. Its ivory handle glows in the firelight.

"You all know our punishment ritual. First the cudgel, then the sacred knife. And tonight we will perform a new ceremony, one used hundreds of years ago to calm angry gods, to ensure the universe would not end. Our efforts will ensure that our small universe, our family, will not end." He pauses, seems to be recalling a pleasant scene. I remember the drops of blood splattering on the carpet at my open door. "Here to observe and then to help us is our visitor, Grandma with the Cart."

Danny's chest moves, and his eyes twitch under their lids. His beard doesn't hide his cheekbones, high like mine used to be, and his long hair is blond under the grime of the matted tails he's worked it into. His eyes will be blue when he opens them.

I feel Jimmy's hand, holding me.

Starkey gives the bat to Jasper. "You have the honor of being first." Jasper gets up slowly, wipes his hands on his pants, takes the bat and aims it. The wood hits an already purple arm with a dull *thud*. He gives the bat to Bebop, who stands over the board and swings at a thigh. Lila gets the bat next and closes her eyes as she goes for the other thigh, and then each kid in succession takes a turn at my son. Danny groans but does not cry out. Perhaps he can't feel anything anymore. I am noticing that none of the blows land on his head or on his ribs.

Then it is my turn.

"I'm an old lady," I say. "I can barely stand up. No way can I swing that thing." I am trying to think what to do. I can't hit Danny. I can't hurt him ever again. "No." I put the bat down at my feet.

Starkey has gotten out of his chair, is standing over me. I twist my neck to look up at him. I can see from this angle that the black smear on his chest is some kind of bird that seems to be staring at me.

"Isn't there another reason why you can't do it, Grandma?"

"Yes," I say. I press my hands on my knees and push myself upright and step back so that I can look past the bird into Starkey's eyes and the feather above them. "This is my son."

"And that is why you'll sit down and listen, Mrs. Miller." His black palm shoves into my chest, and I land hard on a rock in back of me. "Consider this retribution for the time you betrayed your son and, as a consequence, me. Ten years ago. I'm sure you recall that night. We both were forced into hiding after you decided to call the police, teach him a lesson. We have been on the run ever since. But I have been the strong one. I never gave up the power of my anger."

"Jeff? Crazy Jeff? My God." I almost laugh.

CHAPTER FORTY-TWO

MATT

SEPTEMBER 2009

"She said water tower?" Collin sits at Matt's computer, where he has been waiting for his father to get off duty. Tonight they will be shopping for a new laptop for him to take to his college classes, and he is narrowing down his choices in an Internet search. He's hoping for a Mac, Matt knows. However, his father has other things on his mind.

"We'll waste time looking for a duffel. It's almost dark. Even a water tower will be hard to see. We have five thousand acres to search and mostly rabbit paths to follow. Any ideas?" Matt's team has gathered at the table next to his desk.

"Maybe the boundary path?" one of them suggests.

"Same problem. We would be feeling our way down the hills. We could miss the camp by miles."

Matt doesn't know what drove Ellie Miller to attempt to get to the camp. The sight of Sarah at her door, possibly, but the old woman does not seem to be a risk-taker or even slightly impetuous. Except the time she tried to save her son by reporting him. Protective, maybe. He remembers her hand on Sarah's arm, understands that the girl is important to her. So whom is she protecting now that Sarah is being protected by Angie?

"Is it big? The water tower?" Collin asks as his fingers move across the keys of the computer in front of him.

"Yeah, I suppose. I heard it was used a long time ago to collect water for the farm that used to be at the edge of the forest, before the developers moved in and built big houses with views."

"It's probably about eighty years old by now," someone adds. "It's important?" The huddle of cops looks over the shoulder of the intense young man, who stares at the screen in front of him. Matt steps behind Collin and sees what looks like a fuzzy gray cauliflower.

"Wait," Collin says, working the mouse. Then, "See that? That round dot?" His forefinger taps again. The round dot becomes a round structure, then a rough-looking lid, a roof over something.

"The water tower." Collin points at the screen. " 'Peterson Tower,' the label says." He looks up. "Google Earth to the rescue." He continues tapping. "Can't see a duffel, but if we move around, we'll find streets and paths in the area." Names of roads pop up; a wide trail wiggles like a gray snake alongside the water tower. Four men bend closer to the screen.

"West end of the park," one of them says. "Near MacDonald Road."

"But north. I've hiked that trail. You can get to it by parking on Esther Street. Once we're on the trail, we'll pass the tower; then we can head uphill."

"Sarah said to look for smoke." By now Matt is slipping on his holster, pulling on his jacket, and so is his team.

As he follows them, Matt can't resist going to Collin, who is still flying over the park, fascinated with the roof tops of houses at its edge, murmuring, "Look at that mansion! Four cars!"

"Sorry about our plans for tonight, Collin. Grace will be happy to feed you, unless you have other ideas."

Collin's eyes don't leave the screen. "I got it covered, Dad."

As the officers hurry through the front office, Matt catches Shelly's eye. She smiles, says, "Good luck. And if all goes well, I'm planning on seeing you tomorrow. Lunch, remember? My place. Bring Collin if he wants. I'd like to get to know him better."

CHAPTER FORTY-THREE

ELLIE

SEPTEMBER 2009

I look up at this feathered crazy person and see the ten-year-old who came home with Danny one day. They'd met skateboarding on the sidewalk outside, and without a hello, he came in and glanced around our messy house, smirked at the drink in front of me, went to the fridge and looked for something to eat. From that moment on—him scrounging and coming up empty-handed, smiling at me, not really smiling, as he muttered "Shit,"—I disliked him. He was slippery. Always. Smiling one moment, leading Danny away the next.

When they were older, teenagers, I marked my bottles to keep track of how much liquor he was stealing from me. Not Danny, I told myself. I didn't worry much about the beer. At the time I didn't see any harm in it, until the day I came home and found them watching porn, drunk, cans piled in a wobbly pyramid in front of the TV. I yelled. They sent the cans flying all over the room and laughed as they ran out. That was when I understood I was losing my son. A year or so later, Danny left for good.

I have to keep talking, keep him distracted. Maybe one of the kids . . . no, they're as still as the rocks they are hunched on. "You've blamed me for ten years because you did something stupid and almost got caught?"

"Not just you, Mrs. Miller. You, in fact, were only a last straw." Jeff offers me that terrible smile one more time. "No, I blame everyone who has abandoned children—my own father, you, and the parents of children like these."

Uneasy eyes watch us in the orange light. They must be able to see my body shaking under my heavy coat.

"So I learned to build loyal families like this one, taught them the rules of life." He spreads both arms this time, like he's some kind of priest offering a benediction. "I have given these lost children protection and education. At times I might have wanted something in return—love, perhaps—but I soon realized that love is a paltry emotion compared to what I create in my family. Allegiance. Respect.

Safety." He plucks at three fingers, counting his achievements.

"Your son, on the other hand, also blaming you, escaped into drugs, evaporated, a useless derelict. Until this week, when he walked into this camp."

Jeff steps to a rock by the fire, picks up the knife, unsheathes it. "Recognize this, Mrs. Miller? It's yours. The guilt for whatever it has done lies on your shoulders."

It's all coming back, bad scenes flaring like hot sparks from the coals behind me: a sad burned cat left at the building's entry; the little neighbor kid who'd been hung out a window, my window, screaming, "Mommy," his pee dripping on the sidewalk below; the newspapers stuffed into the heat register, set on fire, water from the fire engines pouring through the ceiling into the apartment below; the time the boys were sent home from school for bullying, Jeff laughing, Danny rubbing his bruised knuckles, crying. Me, I was mostly drunk those days, shaking my head; boys will be boys, I said, reaching for my glass. Who knows what else they were up to? Not me. I wasn't there.

"You're crazy. You always were."

"So, Mrs. Miller. Are you surprised that after all these years I recognized you in your sad little disguise? It was the coat, actually, that gave you away, as ugly ten years ago as it is at this moment. Green-and-red plaid, fake-fur collar, you looked like a giant Christmas elf. Danny and I howled. I was glad you weren't my mother."

"So am I."

I was so proud of that bargain coat. $5. When I put it on to show it off, Jeff said the collar looked like roadkill, an opossum, and he turned it up around my face, saying he was looking for babies clinging to its underside. I hung it on an old wire hanger in the coat closet and never wore it again until today.

"Then, of course, there's Smiley. The old man, before he passed out, told the boys and me that a woman took her in, kept her when she was sick. We had to leave before we could find out where this woman lived. I didn't connect you with our lovely girl. So where is she now?"

"I don't know what you're talking about."

He leans over me now, the knife steady in his hand. "No matter. We'll find out sooner or later, Mrs. Miller." He taps Danny on the nose with the blade. I see a flick of blueness. "Hit your son. Right there."

I feel the point of the knife on the back of my neck. I bend down, pick up the bat. My fingers curl around the handle and I'm not thinking anymore.

I lean on the bat to stand up. Then I hold it with both hands, pointing it down at Danny, like I'm practicing, and bring it back up. But instead of aiming it at Danny, I pivot and swing the bat around my knees and against the legs behind me. Jeff laughs. He is so close I can smell him, an ugly, animal odor that somehow sends the pepper-spray can into my hand. I press the button, the spray aimed at his face.

"Fuck!" His palm rubs at his eyes as he lunges at me. I'm thrown to the ground. The weight of his body landing on top of me knocks the wind out of me. A hand reaches out, catches in my hair, and I sense him fumbling for the knife he must have dropped. "You whore!" he screams, his mouth at my ear. "You mother . . . "

I feel the knife enter my shoulder. I'm about to die, and a little surge of joy spurts through me. He's right. I am a mother.

Then he grunts and falls hard against me again, and I can't breathe. Dimly, I feel him being pulled off me. I hear Lila say, "Here, Grandma," as she holds something against the pain in my shoulder.

I push with my good arm to prop myself up, and I see by the firelight that Jeff is lying facedown next to me. A butcher knife with an Italian chef carved into its handle sticks out of his bare back. A dark river meanders along his spine. Around me, a circle is dissolving into fast-moving shadows grabbing at packs and bags, pausing a moment at my feet, whispering good-bye, disappearing into the trees.

Then silence, except for Danny's groans and the startling crack of dry wood as the fire burns down. The shoulder of my old coat is wet with blood, and pain sends me down onto my elbows when I try to stand up. I'm wondering if I will bleed to death before someone finds us. Danny's sounds stop with a low gurgle. Three more deaths for Matt Trommald to investigate, transients all of us.

I lie back down, reach my hand toward the cold fingers of my son, squeeze. Maybe he squeezes back. It doesn't matter. We're together.

The yellow of the last few coals is glowing like a far-away moon, when I hear voices.

"Over here." Flashlights snake around us, blind me. Fingers press against my neck. "She's alive."

"So's this one."

Then I hear Sergeant Trommald's voice talking on his phone, directing ambulances to the road above the park.

"Tell them to look for my cart," I mumble, pleased to be able to help a little. He hears me, touches my cheek.

CHAPTER FORTY-FOUR

ELLIE

OCTOBER 2009

Danny's in my bed this time. After a few days in the hospital, they let him come home if someone is here to give him his pain pills and antibiotics. Someone is. Me, his mother.

"A disguise, Mom," he explains. I'm sitting in the chair next to the bed, listening and pouring ice water when he needs it. "I had to lose what I am, a husband and a father, and turn into a guy working undercover. Took me a while to get the dreads arranged. Part of them is not my own hair." He pulls on one of those ugly tails and teases me. "I kind of like them."

The teasing feels like love. Maybe it also was years before and I didn't get it. "I do, too," I lie. "I'd like them better if they were red or blue. I got food dye."

My son's face is red and blue, and green and purple. So is his body, which I have bathed a couple of times. A man's body, but the warm, soapy washcloth feels the same as it did twenty-eight years ago. "So you were up in Green River and met a girl and got sober."

"That's about it. Only slower. Kristi stuck by me through treatment, my going to school, trying to figure out what I was going to do with my life, when I realized I actually had one. You'll like her."

"When will she come down to get you?"

"When I don't look like a monster. We don't want to alarm Gavin, and I guess I don't want to upset her anymore than she's already been upset. A week or so. So, how good are you at cutting hair?"

"You won't need it for the next job?"

Danny, clean and sober, with a history of homelessness and living in woods, was hired to work in a special division of the Green River police department. Their assignment was to deal with the increase of violence in the town's parks, under freeways, and in vacant buildings.

Transients liked the mild climate and the variety of drugs available in the area, but after several murders of young homeless kids, they got worried, asked for help. Danny was sent out to find what the police imagined were a couple of gangs torturing people for recreation. That search led to McLaughlin and this room.

I don't want to think about the next job. I bet his wife doesn't, either.

"No, I'll be going back to school, I think. Regular law enforcement classes. Living in the woods isn't a good way to be a father."

Father. Shit. I've barely gotten my son back, and now he's someone else's father. I'll have to get used to it. I don't intend to let him go again, even though he's three instead of one. I give him a sip of water. "And Jeff?"

"All we knew up north was that when the murders and abuse seemed to drop off up there, reports came in of similar killings down here in McLaughlin, two hundred miles away. We'd found a dead boy wrapped in a sleeping bag in an abandoned camp; the bag also held the DNA of a murdered girl and her unknown assailant. A few kids talked about the "family" they'd lived with in the forest and how they'd all run away, afraid of the guy who called himself their father. Jeff. They didn't know his last name or anything else about him.

"Then the fingerprints were identified through army records, and I knew we were looking for Jeff.

My Jeff. I was sent down to see if I could find him. I did."

Danny closes his eyes, the meds taking hold again. "You knew he was nuts all along, didn't you? I was pretty stupid."

"Nope. You were just a kid who needed a friend, since you didn't have much of a mother."

And that is how we begin to apologize to each other.

I can't stir or slice with my right arm, it being in a sling. Danny can barely stand up, but he can stir. Together we put together pumpkin pancakes, food bank again, and I find I can turn the cakes over left-handed if I aim carefully. We eat on the bed. I remember eating like this a long time ago when he had the flu and I sat at the foot and he propped himself up at the head and we tried not to spill Lipton noodle soup. Danny remembers, too. He and I have been doing a lot of remembering these past couple of days.

"I was a good mother, some of the time," I say. "I did my best, until the demons took over. Then . . ."

"You did okay, Mom. I was a pretty good son, too, for a long time. Then hormones took over. You weren't so good with the hormones." He laughs. "You never could take a teenage joke."

"The coat, for one? I'm still mad about that, and that coat almost got me, and you, killed."

"No, I was thinking about the time I climbed down the rain spout and went to some girl's house for the night. You saw the open window and thought I'd jumped two and half stories and was lying in the bushes dead."

"Instead you were lying in someone else's bed. No, that wasn't a joke to me."

"Only a kid would see the humor in that."

"What goes around comes around. Better not have rain spouts near Gavin's bedroom a few years from now."

He raises his eyebrows, pretends he's going to watch out for rain spouts. My son, a good man. He tells me that he loves me, that he didn't call these past few years because he wasn't sure how I felt about him. I tell him I wasn't sure either until I saw his broken body, knew that I didn't want to die without asking for his forgiveness.

So we have forgiven each other. And we are learning to laugh and to try not to spill on the bed and to stir and flip for each other.

We have talked to Sarah at the hospital by phone, so when it rings in the hall, I hope that the knock on the door means it's a call for me, for us. The super nods and points and smiles. He is pleased to have heroes in his building. He has forgotten that I have given him notice. "It's Sarah."

"I'm getting better," she says in answer to my first question. "I'm talking to a nice lady who works with raped women. I'm still in shock, I guess, but not so much. She says we'll keep talking for a while, maybe a group, to help me with my dreams, even after I leave here."

I have dreams, too. I'll get over mine on my own, as usual, but I'm glad for her. "Good," I say. "When do you get to leave?" I am not considering what my question means. It is my insides doing the asking.

"I guess I'll be going to a group home. That's what we talked about today."

"And?" I am praying, if you can call it that, for her to ask the next question.

"I'm wondering." She may be crying. Knowing her, I know she's crying.

"What?"

"Maybe if I can stay with you? I don't know . . . "

"Yes," I say. "Somehow we'll . . ."

Now I'm crying, just a little. I don't want it to become a habit. The super is standing a few doors away, listening, I'm sure.

"Oh, Ellie. I can't wait to come home."

And two days later she does. Now I have a beat-up son on the davenport, and a beat-up girl in the bed, and I'm sleeping in the Barcalounger some renter has left behind and the super has lent me. Until I move. *We* move.

We have canned ham, even though it is past the eat-now-or-never date for most folks. We also are cooking boxed mashed potatoes, baked squash, overflow from a local organic garden, and warming a pie from an upscale restaurant that donates gourmet leftovers to volunteers who pick it up, deliver it to the food bank. A feast.

Danny is still on injury furlough, but he's going home tomorrow. His wife has been advised of the leveling-off of his purple-turned-greenness and scabs. She is anxious to welcome him back. This is the longest time he has been away since Gavin was born, since he went undercover. She's hoping, she says, he gets a desk job when he's officially on the force. He's looking, though, as he repeats her words to me, as if he's ready for a rainspout escape. They'll work it out.

I've bought a bottle of sparkling apple juice. We are sipping, munching on a pile of off-date trail mix. We have questions.

Sarah first. "Someone stabbed him—good riddance. Does anyone know who?"

"Absolute secrecy?" I ask.

She rolls her eyes yes.

"I have no idea. The knife was from my kitchen, yes. It was in my pocket, yes. I was flat on my stomach when it was used."

"You must have an idea." This Sarah will make it to college.

"Secrecy? Like I never said this?"

Eye roll.

"Jimmy was on one side of me, his hand on my knee to shut me up. Leaky was on a blanket at my feet, like a guardian angel, kind of. Everyone else was so petrified they were probably sh . . . "

"Mom. Conjecture. Facts, please." Danny is back to being a policeman.

"No one moved. Better?"

"And?"

"When I swung the bat, I felt someone in my pocket, pushing the pepper spray can at me. I felt someone in my other pocket, pulling out the knife whose point had been making a hole in my leg. I may have dreamed all this." I didn't.

"One of their talents was pickpocketing," Sarah says.

"Maybe still is."

"Someone also knew enough to wipe the prints off the belly of the fat little chef." Mine and someone else's. Danny raises a glass to me, to a smart kid, as he catches my eye.

"Where are they?" Far, far away, I hope.

"Sergeant Trommald . . . " Danny begins.

"Matt," I correct. We're definitely on a first-name basis after all this activity.

"Matt said that Jimmy and Leaky are in a safe house, a kind of shelter for kids who will be in court, maybe in legal danger. They claim they don't know who stabbed Starkey. Bebop and Jasper disappeared the night it all happened. Owl is now in a place for people like her, social worker and all. Goose is somewhere on the street; I guess she's eighteen, on her own."

"Lila?" I kind of admired her in her finery. Of course she is with Mouse somewhere.

"She's back at home. Her grandma's. She's waiting for Mouse to show up. It might be a long wait."

We think about these kids, the ways they've scattered in just a few days, the separate ways we're going also, even as we sit here drinking sparkling cider.

"A family is pretty important for growing up, isn't it?" Danny says.

And for growing old, I want to add.

"Jeff understood that much earlier than I did. I guess that's why . . . " Danny is quiet for a minute, then keeps going. "I knew it. I just didn't know how to get back to mine, and he had none to get back to."

A knock. Matt comes in, settles down on the davenport, accepts a glass of cider. He's been by a couple of times. One time he brought his son, a brilliant tech guy, Matt said, starting college. His son didn't say much, just smiled at his father when Matt mentioned his help in finding the camp. He looked a little anxious to leave after a few minutes. I like that Matt shared his family with us, like we share ours with him. We'll maybe be friends when things are all settled down.

We always have questions for him. This time he has questions for us. He looks at Danny. "I've been wondering. How did you know where to find Jeff in the forest?"

Danny shrugs. "The night Jeff and I ran away, we camped near there. It was a place we had done drugs at, even had a stash hidden about where the tent was—gone of course, by the time we decided to head north. I talked to a few street kids, and rumors of this Starkey person living in the county forest kept coming up. I wandered along the paths until I smelled the smoke and heard voices. And there he was. My old friend. Crazy as hell. Probably a murderer." He shakes his head like he still can't quite believe it.

Matt's glass is empty.

"More?" I move to get the bottle.

"Sorry, I'm actually here to ask you for something." He stands, upper lip moist, not looking at me.

"What?" But I know, and it's in the just-taken-away garbage.

"Your coat. I need to look at it."

"We all hated that old coat. Bought it at Goodwill ten or more years ago for five dollars. My son laughed at it. I decided it was time to get rid of it. It's in the bottom of a Waste Management truck headed for Idaho, or wherever we send our trash." I make my eyes wide and innocent, and he takes a big breath. He and I both understand what a hole in the bottom of one pocket and a small scar on my leg probably means. The other pocket is innocent. Pepper spray doesn't kill people.

"One more thing. Can I check your knife drawers, Ellie? My team seems to think that knives like the one that killed Jeff came with a carving fork, same design. I told them I'd look when I came by." He sends me an *I'm sorry* shit-faced look.

This could complicate our happy ending. The fork with another fat Italian chef on its handle is somewhere. Where? "Don't you need a piece of paper to search my stuff?" I ask. The frown on Matt's face tells me I sound guilty as sin.

"It's okay," Danny says. "Let him look. It's part of his job."

So I do. He rattles through my drawers. No fork. Matt thanks us, says that will probably do it, as far as the investigation goes. He'll see us again, soon, he promises, when this is all over. Then, as he goes out the door, he turns to Danny, shakes his hand. "It's been interesting working with you. I hope we can do it again."

And I realize that Matt knew Danny was on the trail of a killer, was in town, was undercover, maybe even as he asked me how my son was doing.

"The fork's also on the way to Idaho," Danny says when I ask. "Along with the coat. You and I make a good team."

CHAPTER FORTYFIVE

SARAH

OCTOBER 2009

Ellie and I went shopping for a new sofa bed today. We just moved into our new apartment, two floors above where she used to live, which made moving stuff a lot easier since the super is happy to keep us in the building, and he helped. The new apartment has two bedrooms, and they'll deliver the sofa bed, and a new mattress set for our second bedroom, which will be mine, tomorrow. When Danny and his family come down to visit, I'll share with Gavin, and Danny and his wife will sleep in the living room, or vice versa. Doesn't matter. We'll all have a bed. Christmas, probably.

Ellie is sitting on the floor making a list. "We need dishes and glasses if we're going to have the family here. And sheets, new towels, and a new shower curtain, maybe one of those guaranteed not to mildew."

She's still writing things down, and I ask her how we can afford all this new stuff. "I'm spending my retirement instead of leaving it to my children," she answers. "All one thousand dollars of it. Besides, I'm going to work, part-time. I'm going to be a graffiti inspector, take pictures of the tags and graffiti all around this part of town."

Ellie waves her arm, the good one, and grins. "It'll help when taggers are caught; fifteen offenses, and they're off to juvie." She hesitates, maybe remembering threatening someone else with those words a long time ago. "Well, probably not juvie, but definitely community service. Matt came up with this job." Then she hunches up on one arm, presses her knees against the floor, and pulls herself up.

"Let's go shopping," she says. "We both need new shoes."

The End

CPSIA information can be obtained at www.ICGtesting.com
Printed in the USA
LVOW01s0001100114

368858LV00013B/218/P